"I thought you n̶...
He held up the s...

"Well, thank you," she said as she reached for the pink material, "but I can take care of myself."

Drew didn't doubt it. Debbie had been on her own since her mother died. "I know you can. But once in a while, it's nice to have someone take care of you."

Sliding the shawl from her hands, he draped the material over her shoulders, keeping hold of both ends. "Maybe," she conceded. "But I don't need—"

"This isn't about need," he interrupted. "It's about want."

Debbie swallowed. "Want?"

"It's like...dessert. Not something you need but certainly something you crave."

"And let me guess. You're craving something *sweet.*" The sardonic twist on the word told Drew what Debbie thought of that description—one he'd been guilty of using in the past.

"I was thinking more along the lines of something rich, decadent, a little sinful even."

Debbie's eyes widened, huge and sparkling in the faint light streaming through the French doors. He'd gone too far, he thought.

* * *

THE PIRELLI BROTHERS:
These California boys know what love is all about!

Dear Reader,

It's always a thrill to get emails from readers—especially when they ask about secondary characters in previous books. I've had more than a few asking when Drew Pirelli would get his own story...and here it is!

As the middle brother, Drew has always been the mediator and peacemaker in his family. He's a somewhat serious and settled kind of guy who's not big on change. So imagine his surprise when he starts to see his longtime friend, Debbie Mattson, as more than the girl next door.

Debbie feels she's spent too much of her life serious and settled. She's looking for fun and excitement and for a guy who is someone new, someone different—someone very much *un*like Drew.

I have to admit, I didn't plan for these two to end up as a couple, but the more I thought about it, the more I realized just how perfect they are for each other. It's been a fun journey to see these friends who've known each other their whole lives realize they still have so much more to learn.

I hope you enjoy *Small-Town Cinderella* and please look for my next book, coming in early 2015, in which local cowboy Jarrett Deeks and city cousin Theresa Pirelli seek a happily-ever-after of their own.

Happy reading!

Stacy Connelly

Small-Town Cinderella

—

Stacy Connelly

HHARLEQUIN®SPECIAL EDITION®

Recycling programs
for this product may
not exist in your area.

ISBN-13: 978-0-373-65832-9

SMALL-TOWN CINDERELLA

Printed in U.S.A.

Books by Stacy Connelly

Harlequin Special Edition

Her Fill-In Fiancé #2128
Temporary Boss...Forever Husband #2148
Darcy and the Single Dad #2237
Daddy Says, "I Do!" #2250
Small-Town Cinderella #2350

Silhouette Special Edition

All She Wants for Christmas #1944
Once Upon a Wedding #1992
The Wedding She Always Wanted #2033

*The Pirelli Brothers

Other books by Stacy Connelly available in ebook format.

STACY CONNELLY

has dreamed of publishing books since she was a kid, writing stories about a girl and her horse. Eventually, boys made it onto the page as she discovered a love of romance and the promise of happily ever after.

When she is not lost in the land of make-believe, Stacy lives in Arizona with her two spoiled dogs. She loves to hear from readers and can be contacted at stacyconnelly@cox.net or www.stacyconnelly.com.

To the staff at The Red Garter Bed & Breakfast
in Williams, Arizona. Thanks for answering
my questions about running a small-town bakery.

Chapter One

"To the newlywed and the two brides-to-be," Debbie Mattson said as she raised her margarita to her friends. "May you always be as lucky in life as you have been in love."

Darcy Dawson, the bachelorette of their party, lifted her green-apple martini. "To luck and life and love," she echoed.

The four women—Debbie, Darcy, Sophia Pirelli Cameron and the newest member of the group, Kara Starling—had gathered at The Clearville Bar and Grille for Darcy's final send-off as a single woman. The rustic bar was a favorite locale for tourists and townies alike with its flatscreen televisions for the sports lovers and small dance floor for music lovers. Had Debbie been in charge of the bachelorette party, she might have tried for something a little more exciting than dinner and drinks, but Darcy was clearly having a good time, and that was all that mattered.

Six months pregnant, dark-haired Sophia sipped at her own cranberry juice. If Debbie had ever seen a woman with a pregnancy glow, it was her friend, who looked adorable in a floral skirt and long-sleeved pink peasant blouse draped over her round belly. Of course, it just as easily could have been a newlywed glow, as Sophia had married Jake Cameron the previous summer.

Love clearly agreed with Sophia and seemed to be first and foremost on her mind as she exchanged a glance with Darcy and Kara before looking over at Debbie. "With the three of us already finding our guys, you know what that means, right? It's your turn now."

Debbie held on to her smile even though she groaned inside. How many times had she heard that over the past few months? Ever since her friends had met their soul mates, they'd set their sights on the only single member left in their circle. At times, she felt very much the lone sheep about to be set upon by wolves. Cunning, devious, *matchmaking* wolves.

Show no fear, she thought to herself, knowing if she wavered even slightly she was dead meat.

"I'm happy for all of you, I really am. But I'm nowhere near ready to settle down. I'm finally at a place in my life where I have time to look for a little adventure and excitement."

"And romance?" Darcy chimed in slyly.

"I wouldn't be opposed to having, oh, say…a red-hot fling." Debbie took another sip of her margarita, the salty, tart combination making her taste buds tingle while the alcohol warmed her to her subject. "With a guy who's dark and mysterious and exciting, who'll ride into town and sweep me off my feet. Someone who'll take me completely by surprise and keep me on my toes."

"Now you're talking," the gorgeous redhead said with a grin.

"Excuse me?" Kara protested, using a look her friends had dubbed her "professor glare." "Need I remind you that you're getting married this weekend?"

Lifting up her hands in an innocent gesture she couldn't quite pull off while still holding her martini glass, the bride-to-be retorted, "All the more reason to live vicariously through Debbie's escapades. So tell us more about this mystery man."

Feeling heat rush to her face, Debbie set aside her margarita. "Well, I can tell you one thing. I'm certainly not going to find him here," she said wryly.

"At the bar?" Kara asked.

"Not here at the bar. Not here in Clearville." A quick glance around their section of the restaurant confirmed what Debbie already expected.

She knew every single guy in the place. More than that, even; she'd known them all for years. If she thought back, she could picture any number of their embarrassing, awkward moments that were part and parcel of growing up in a small town.

Billy Cummings, the sheriff's son, had gone on a football kick after seeing his first professional game and had worn a miniature helmet 24/7 for weeks on end. Mark Thompson had had the biggest crush on their freshman English teacher, and his brother, Bruce, swore the garage band he was in would make it big even though none of the members could actually play an instrument. Then there was Darrell Nelson and the cruel pranks he used to play, bullying anyone who was smaller and weaker than he was.

She remembered it all, and if that wasn't bad enough, she was well aware they remembered all the awkward growing pains she'd gone through, too.

Mystery? Romance? Excitement?

Not a chance, she thought with a sigh.

"Look, just forget everything I said. This is what happens when a milk-and-cookies girl starts hitting the tequila and lime," she joked, hoping her friends would be as willing to laugh off her comments.

She should have known she wouldn't be so lucky.

"There's nothing wrong with wanting some romance in your life," Kara told her.

At first, Debbie had wondered about the quietly serious college professor marrying Sophia's fun-loving, outgoing brother Sam. But over the past few weeks, Debbie had gotten to know Kara and to see the warm heart behind the classy blonde's cool exterior.

"And I highly recommend having a gorgeous guy sweep you off your feet." Darcy grinned. "But why are you totally discounting the whole Clearville male population? I speak from personal experience when I say my guy is anything but boring."

"I'll drink to that," Kara said as she lifted her glass of chardonnay to tap against Darcy's appletini.

Their smiles shone with newfound love, though Debbie had a hard time picturing Nick and Sam Pirelli as romantic, sweep-a-girl-off-her-feet types. They'd always been more like big brothers to her—sometimes sweet, sometimes annoying, always overprotective big brothers.

That was something Sophia as the youngest Pirelli and only girl could certainly understand. After exchanging a look with her friend, Debbie argued, "It's different for the two of you. Neither of you grew up here, so to you, Clearville guys are mysterious and exciting. But for me, these are the guys I've known forever. The boys next door. No mystery, no excitement, no sparks."

All that was bad enough. Worse was knowing the male

population of the town viewed her the same way. The girl next door. The buddy, the pal, the friend whose shoulder they cried on when the popular, pretty girls turned them down.

She winced at the memory when she thought of the name that had followed her since her days at Redwood Elementary School, thanks in part to the bakery her mother owned and the sweets that had filled her lunches and helped fill out her waistline. She'd never been "little" anything, and while she'd known the nickname was mostly a lighthearted tease, it had hurt all the same.

Now she was the owner of Bonnie's Bakery, and the years of taking care of her mother after she'd fallen ill and spending all her free time at the bakery had toughened her like overkneaded dough. Her feelings weren't so easily injured anymore, though she'd suffered a setback thanks to her last boyfriend.

She and Robert Watkins had dated casually for several months earlier in the year, and things had finally started to get serious over the summer. Serious enough for them to sleep together.

Debbie still wasn't sure which was worse, the pain of heartbreak or the pain of humiliation as she remembered that fateful weekend, and how he'd picked the very next day to tell her he thought they'd be better off just being friends.

It wouldn't have been so bad if the breakup hadn't dragged her back to her high school insecurities. To being every guy's friend, the buddy they could talk to about the prettier, more popular girls they liked. She thought she'd gotten over that. She *was* over it. But Debbie couldn't pretend the split with Robert hadn't brought back a lot of bad memories.

Memories she was determined to overcome. She was

woman enough to have confidence in herself, to know what she wanted and to go after it.

"I'm not sure you're giving these guys enough credit," Darcy argued. "There are some nice men around here who'd be thrilled to know you're looking for a boyfriend." Her eyes lit suddenly. "What about Jarrett Deeks? He and Nick have gotten to be friends working together at Jarrett's horse rescue. We could set up a double date if you want."

Debbie cringed slightly at the thought. "No, thank you, Darcy. I'm sure Jarrett's great and all, but a double date isn't exactly what I had in mind."

Her friend's brow furrowed. "But if you're looking for a relationship—"

"I'm not," she interrupted. "Not really."

"A not-really relationship?" Kara echoed.

"I'm not looking for anything that serious." Debbie stabbed her straw at the ice cubes lingering at the bottom of her glass. "I just want to have some fun." Leaning back against the padded booth, she said, "I feel like I missed out on so much growing up, you know?"

"Actually, we don't." Kara leaned forward, her expression open and interested. "You talk a lot without saying much about yourself."

Debbie blinked, startled by her friend's comment. "I don't do that…do I?" She knew she liked to talk, and the more nervous she became, the more she said—often without saying much at all. But she didn't like to think she fell into that pattern even with her friends. It sounded…selfish. Like she expected them to open their hearts and spill their guts while she kept all her emotions inside. "I'm sorry. I didn't realize—"

"Sweetie, it's not a criticism. Just a comment."

"And I do know what you mean, Deb," Sophia interjected as she shifted forward in the booth as far as her pregnant belly would allow. "So many of us grew up together that we don't go around talking about past history because everyone knows everything."

"But we're new." Darcy's nod included Kara as she added, "So you can tell us all your old stories without worrying that we've heard them before."

"Well, okay, but just because you haven't heard it all before doesn't mean it isn't still boring. My dad was in the military and was killed overseas when I was really young, so growing up, it was just me and my mom. I was still in high school when she was diagnosed with cancer."

Debbie could still remember walking into the bakery after school that day, the scent of vanilla and chocolate strong in the air. She'd been so excited. Posters had decorated the hall for the homecoming dance, and she'd been so sure that that year someone would ask her to go. She even had the perfect dress picked out, her teenage head filled with plans for the future.

"I could tell right away something was wrong, and when she told me— It was like a nightmare. Something that couldn't be true. But it was."

Clearing her throat, she said, "Anyway, my mom always was a fighter, so she went through all the tests and surgeries and treatments, all while still trying to run the bakery. For a while, I thought about dropping out of school, but she wouldn't hear of it. I took as few classes as I could to get by, quit all extracurricular activities, and I worked in the bakery every spare second I had. A few hours before school and then from the minute I got out until close."

She'd never bought that dress. Had never attended that homecoming dance or any other dance in high school. The bakery became Debbie's life the way it had always been her mother's before that.

"It was all I could do.… I couldn't make her better, but

I could make the cupcakes," she concluded with a watery laugh.

Shaking off the sorrows of the past, she protested, "This is not the conversation for a bachelorette party! Here I'm talking about wanting to have fun, and yet I'm the one bringing everyone down."

"You aren't. I think what you did was amazing, and I know a little of what you went through," Darcy confided.

Debbie knew her friend had lost her mother a few years ago. It was that loss that had prompted Darcy to move to her mother's hometown and open the beauty shop the two of them had always dreamed of owning. Darcy had shared that with Debbie not long after they met, and yet she hadn't thought to confide in her friend about her own past, despite what the two of them had in common. Was it like Sophia said, and Debbie simply expected everyone to already know her life story, or was there more to it?

Saving that thought for another time, Debbie said, "Thank you, but it didn't feel like much. Still, I knew how much the bakery meant to my mom, and I did all I could to keep the doors open so she could concentrate on getting better. And for a while, she did. The cancer went into remission for a few years before it came back, but the second time there was no fighting it."

And after her mother had passed away, it was just Debbie and the bakery. Working long hours to numb the sense of loss and to slowly accept the bakery now *was* her future. The dreams she'd had in high school of attending culinary school and becoming a chef had slipped way as she'd kneaded dough and rolled out cookies and decorated cupcakes. But somehow, as those hours turned into days and weeks and years, a minor miracle had taken place.

The reputation of the small-town shop had grown. Business had increased thanks to Debbie establishing an online presence. Now her loyal customers didn't have to wait for their yearly trip to the tourist town to order her desserts. They could cater to their craving for something sweet with a few clicks of a mouse, and Debbie could ship her cookies and cheesecakes straight to their door.

She'd even gained the attention of *Just Desserts* magazine. The article had praised her double-chocolate cake and strawberry-filled vanilla cupcakes. As pleased as she was with the recognition, Debbie couldn't help feeling like, well, a fraud. Those were her mother's recipes, and Bonnie should have been the one to bask in the glow of the reporter's praise.

But the article, along with the increase in business, had inspired Debbie to hire on more help. Over the years, she'd frequently paid local teens to run the front register. But Kayla Walker, a young mother who'd moved to Clearville with her boyfriend after she'd inherited a house from her late grandfather, was the first employee Debbie had trained to do the actual baking.

Thanks to Kayla, Debbie now had the chance to expand the menu a bit. To offer her mother's tried-and-true recipes as well as some not-so-vanilla recipes of her own. And with the rush of engagements lately, she was also getting the opportunity to shift her attention from everyday cupcakes and muffins to once-in-a-lifetime wedding cakes.

Working with the bride and groom to find the perfect flavor and filling combinations was a challenge she enjoyed. And then there was the decorating—the literal icing on the cake. The creativity and artistry of building the multiple layers, of designing the perfect flowers and ribbons and scrollwork… She loved every step of the detailed work.

And while she might be a complete flop when it came to love and romance, that didn't mean she wasn't a believer in other couples' happily ever afters. Her friends were all proof that loves of a lifetime did exist, and while Debbie couldn't be more pleased, she wasn't looking to join them.

For the first time in nearly a decade, she had time. Time to think, to breathe, to hang up her apron and have some fun. And if her mother's death had taught her anything, it was that life was short, and Debbie was determined to make the most of it.

"So maybe that's why I'm not looking to settle down," she concluded. "I've been too settled already, too serious and dedicated throughout what should have been the best years of my life. I know the three of you have found the guys of your dreams, and I'm happy for you all, but that's just not what I'm looking for."

"Debbie wants Mr. Excitement," Sophia said with a wink.

"Mr. Mysterious," Darcy seconded.

"Here's to finding Mr. Tall, Dark and Handsome," Kara added.

Still feeling a little ridiculous for spelling out her dream man to her friends, Debbie lifted her glass. "I will definitely drink to that."

Draining the last of her margarita, she admitted finding an exciting and mysterious man was only half the wish. Finding a man who thought *she* was exciting and mysterious…now, *that* would be a fantasy come true.

Drew Pirelli was not a man given to eavesdropping. Living in Clearville his whole life, he was very familiar with its grapevine and the wildfire spread of small-town gossip. He preferred to mind his own business with the somewhat vain hope others would do the same. Neither was he the type to spy on his sister and future sisters-in-law.

If he'd known drinks at the bar and grill were part of the plan for Darcy's bachelorette party, he would have stayed

away. Far away. But he'd been somewhat out of the Pirelli family loop recently, something his parents had commented on more than once. He'd used work as a handy
excuse, and he *was* busy running his construction company, but that was only part of the reason why he'd avoided
family gatherings recently.

How was it, he wondered, that he was the last unattached Pirelli sibling?

Ever since the custom-home side of his business had
taken off, Drew had started each project with his own future family in mind. He pictured his wife and family gathered together in the kitchen. His kids watching television
or playing games in the den. The woman he loved welcoming him to bed in the spacious master suite.

And yet at the end of each project, he turned the keys
over to some other man who would live with his wife and
children in the house Drew had painstakingly built.

The nagging dissatisfaction of giving away a piece of
himself in each of his houses had convinced him to start
building his own place. But that had created another frustration. His attention to detail, the dream of making a
house into *his* home, had helped Drew cement his reputation as one of the most sought-after contractors in North-
ern California. Because of that, he was having trouble
finding time to work on his own project while managing
the custom-home business as well as the rental cabins he
was currently building for Jarrett Deeks.

Not that it was all bad. Professionally, he was as rock
solid as the houses he built. On a personal level, though,
he couldn't seem to find his footing.

And that was the real reason he'd been keeping his
distance from his family. He was tired of being the third,
fifth, heck, even the ninth wheel, depending on how many
of his relatives showed up.

Which was how he'd ended up completely out of the loop when it came to Darcy's bachelorette party.

When he'd first recognized the female voices coming from the other side of the half wall separating the two rows of booths, he'd slid across the padded seat, ready to slip away unnoticed. Though no expert at bachelorette parties, he knew enough to realize guys weren't allowed.

But before he could push to his feet, the words drifting over from the other side of the booth nailed him to the spot.

I wouldn't be opposed to having a red-hot fling with a guy who's dark and mysterious and exciting, who'll ride into town and sweep me off my feet. Someone who'll take completely by surprise and keep me on my toes.

It wasn't the words that had knocked his feet out from under him. It was shock at the swift, unexpected kick of desire he felt when he heard them.

Drew had known Debbie Mattson her entire life. His earliest memories of her were of her standing on tiptoe to peek up over the counter at her mother's bakery, her big blue eyes sparkling as she flashed her dimples at every customer to walk through the door. She was the typical girl next door. Sweet, friendly, cute. She was his kid sister's friend, but her words pointed out a truth he'd been denying for the past several months.

Debbie wasn't a kid anymore.

His knuckles whitened around the cool glass bottle, and he couldn't remember the last time he'd had to fight so hard not to follow his first instinct. An instinct logic told him was completely irrational. If he did what he longed to do, opened his mouth and spouted off like some kind of idiot about nice girls staying home and waiting for the right kind of guy to come along, Debbie would likely knock his block off, and he'd deserve it.

Debbie was a grown woman now. A beautiful woman,

he was reminded as he thought back to Sophia's wedding a few months earlier.

The wedding had been a small affair, with the reception held in their parents' backyard. Already a few months pregnant at the time, his sister had wanted to keep things quiet and low-key. She'd still felt a little insecure about returning home after leaving town five years before following a break-in at The Hope Chest, the local antiques shop she now managed. Though Sophia hadn't been involved in the burglary and vandalism, she'd taken the blame. Feelings of guilt had kept her away until their parents' anniversary party brought her back—with her former boyfriend, Jake Cameron, hot on her heels.

Like the rest of the family, Drew had been happy his sister had fallen in love with a good man who was clearly in love with her. The day of the wedding, Sophia had looked beautiful in her off-white gown with pale pink roses woven into her dark hair, and her new husband hadn't been able to take his eyes off her.

But it was Debbie, Sophia's maid of honor, who kept drawing Drew's attention. Something she'd evidently noticed as their gazes met before she made her way across lush green lawn. The pale pink gown hugged her curves and left the fair skin of her shoulders and arms bare. Her blond hair was caught up in a cascade of ringlets, and her blue eyes glittered in the white lights strung between the trees. "You should know, Drew, my money's on you."

"Excuse me?"

"The bet on whether you or Sam will be the next to fall," Debbie said, referring to his younger, footloose brother.

"Seriously? People are placing bets?"

"You better believe it," she retorted. "And my money's on you all the way. Sam's not the type to settle down while you, well, you're about as settled as any guy I've ever met."

"Sorry, Debbie, I couldn't tell. Was that an insult or a compliment?"

Tipping her head back, she gave a boisterous laugh guaranteed to turn every male head her way. "Oh, that was a compliment. If I decide to insult you, trust me when I say you'll feel it."

"So you think I'm settled?" he asked, falling back on the teasing, brotherly attitude that had long marked their relationship, even as he felt that balance start to shift in a way he couldn't explain.

"You're as grounded as a man can be and still manage to move both feet."

At the time, her teasing comments hadn't bothered him. Much. But now Debbie's voice reached inside him and threatened to shake something loose. The excitement, the anticipation, the "what if" underscoring her words struck a chord inside him that had been still and silent far too long.

But Debbie wasn't the woman who should be striking those notes. She was a friend, a good friend, and thinking of her in any other way just seemed…wrong. For Drew, dating had always been something of a game, a battle of the sexes he only engaged in on a level playing field. He liked women who were sophisticated and experienced and not the type to have their hearts easily broken. Women very unlike Debbie, who, despite the girl talk going on one booth over, had a tender and innocent heart she hid behind a smart mouth and sassy smile.

The hell of it was that he liked her. A lot. Too much, maybe, for him to ask her out and risk Debbie getting hurt. And getting hurt was exactly what might happen if she was serious about going after her mysterious stranger.

Judging from the sounds coming from the other booth, the women were getting ready to leave. Drew set his beer aside and half rose, ready to circle around to the other side of the restaurant and tell Debbie—what, exactly? That she shouldn't—couldn't—go after the adventure and excitement she was looking for?

She was young, beautiful, single. After the years of caring for her mother and running the bakery, she had every right to go after what she wanted. Any man would jump at the chance to fulfill the longing he'd heard in Debbie's voice.

Or more like any *other* man because Drew just didn't think of Debbie that way.

Did he?

"Are you sure you don't want us to give you a ride?" Sophia asked as the four women stepped out of the bar onto the quiet street. For obvious reasons, she was the designated driver and was in charge of seeing Darcy and Kara safely home.

"I only live five minutes away." She'd lived her entire life in a small apartment above the bakery. As a teenager, she'd longed for more space and room of her own, but after her mother passed away, the two-bedroom unit had been more than large enough, at times seeming far too empty. "The night air will help clear my head."

Debbie knew her limit and had stopped after her second margarita. The first had loosened her tongue more than she wanted to admit. She could only hope the drinks the other women had enjoyed would help them forget some of the foolish things she'd said.

"All right. But if you meet up with any dark handsome strangers on the way home, don't do anything I wouldn't do."

No such luck with her perfectly sober best friend. "Can you please forget I said anything?"

Sophia grinned impishly, reminding Debbie of when

they'd been kids, always looking for some kind of trouble. "Not a chance."

With a put-upon sigh, Debbie looked over at the bride-to-be. "Have a good night, Darcy, and just think, the next time we're all together, you'll be a few hours away from becoming Mrs. Nick Pirelli."

The redhead's beaming smile could have lit the sky. "I can't wait!"

Leaving her friends with a wave goodbye, Debbie walked the quiet street toward the bakery. The night was cold with a definite hint of fall in the air, along with woodsmoke drifting from a nearby chimney. Halloween decorations lurked in the shadows behind the darkened windows, reminding Debbie the holiday was less than a month away.

She wasn't sure when she first noticed the sound of footsteps behind her. With the bar only a few doors back, it wasn't that unusual to think someone else had decided to walk off a beer or two. But the late hour and emptiness of the stores around her was enough to quicken her pace. Most nights she would have circled around to the alleyway behind the bakery and the outside staircase that led directly to her apartment. But tonight, the security lights inside the shop beckoned with the promise of safety.

Reaching inside her oversize bag, she fumbled for her keys. Why couldn't she be one of those women who carried a purse the size of a cell phone case? Instead she'd fallen in love with a tapestry-style tote and stuffed it to the zipper with every item she might ever need. Her finger brushed a metal ring, but her relief was short-lived as she identified the extra set of measuring spoons she'd somehow misplaced. Swearing beneath her breath, she looked inside her bag and spotted the pink enamel cupcake-shaped key ring Sophia had given for her last birthday.

Her heart skipped a beat as she heard a sound behind her—"Debbie! Wait up!"

Stumbling, she glanced back over her shoulder toward the familiar voice. "Drew? What do you think you're doing!" she demanded as he jogged toward her. Her heart still pounding, she reached out and socked him on the arm. The muscled bicep felt rock solid against her knuckles, and he didn't even flinch. "You nearly gave me a heart attack!"

The dim lighting from the shop windows illuminated his frown. "I called your name like three times."

He had? "Oh, sorry. I guess I wasn't paying attention."

"And that's the problem. You should be paying attention. Walking home by yourself—"

Swallowing a sigh, she tuned out the rest of what he was saying. Clearly with Sophia now married with a husband to take care of her, Drew had decided to move his big-brother act down the road and to her door.

Debbie had long thought Sophia's middle brother was the most handsome of the three very good-looking men. She'd even had a crush on him once upon a time when she'd been a starry-eyed kid experiencing her first rush of romance. Or hormones, she thought ruefully, still slightly embarrassed by the tongue-tied, blushing preteen she'd once been. But that was a long time ago, and she was over him.

Still, that didn't stop a few of those long-buried feelings from shaking off a bit of dust as she gazed up at him in the moonlight. Even casually dressed like just about every local guy, in a gray henley shirt tucked into faded jeans and a denim jacket to ward off the chill stretched across his broad shoulders, something about Drew made him stand out from the crowd. It was more than looks—although he was…so…good-looking. Totally unfair, in fact, for a man to be that gorgeous.

How many times had she imagined running her fingers through the waves in his dark hair? Pictured how his brown eyes would darken with passion in the seconds before he kissed her? Wondered what it would be like to feel his body pressed against hers?

How many hours had she wasted, her mind taunted her, since Drew would never think of her in the same way?

Slapping those old memories aside, Debbie cut off the rest of his lecture, insisting, "I can take care of myself, Drew. I'm a big girl now."

Was it her imagination or had his gaze dropped slightly at her words, giving her a subtle once-over? She didn't have many opportunities to dress up, and the bachelorette party had given her an excuse to wear her new cream slacks and the wide-necked gold sweater that hugged her curves and, yes, she'd admit it, showed off a fair amount of cleavage. She'd pulled on her leather jacket before leaving the bar, but the blazer style only had a single button, which emphasized rather than hid her figure.

Not that Drew would notice. Her heart skipped a beat. Would he?

"All the more reason to be careful," he warned, his voice gruffer than a moment before. Enough to make her wonder. "A woman like you—"

"A woman like me?"

"A beautiful woman like you needs to be careful. There are guys out there who would take advantage."

Debbie's mind was too caught up on his first words—Drew thought she was beautiful?—to pay attention to whatever else it was he was so intent on telling her. And as he walked her the rest of the way home, a solid masculine presence at her side, she couldn't help wondering what it would be like if Drew was one of those guys. The kind to take advantage at the end of a date by pushing for a good-night kiss and maybe even more.

Her skin heated, and she could only bless the moonlight for hiding her reaction to the thought. Because of course this wasn't a date, and as they reached the bakery door, she reminded him, "This is Clearville, Drew. I know pretty much all the guys 'out there.'"

His jaw clenched as if holding back whatever else he wanted to say. And despite her claim of knowing all there was to know about Clearville guys, his dark eyes were glittering in a way that was completely…unfamiliar.

"Maybe," he finally conceded as he reached out for her keys, "but you never know what might happen…even in a small town like this."

His hand closed over hers, and Debbie's breath caught in her chest. The stroke of his thumb against her skin combined with the deep rumble of his voice sent a shiver down her spine. Surely not what he intended. He was warning her, wasn't he? Trying to scare her…not trying to seduce her.

Heart pounding, her mouth was suddenly too dry to swallow and her tongue snuck out to dampen her lips. Drew tracked the movement, the small amount of moisture evaporating as he leaned closer…

Turning the key in the lock, he pushed the door open and stepped back. "Good night, Debbie. Sweet dreams."

His parting words stayed with her long after she'd climbed the stairs to the safety of her apartment and locked the door behind her. Sweet dreams? With her hand still tingling from his touch, Debbie knew Drew had just about guaranteed he would play a starring role in hers!

Chapter Two

"Don't they make such a lovely couple?"

Debbie looked away from the just-married couple in question to meet Vanessa Pirelli's smiling expression. Nick and Darcy were supposed to be posing for pictures beside the three-tiered wedding cake, but from what Debbie could see, the two of them appeared completely oblivious as they gazed into each other's eyes. The love between them radiated as brightly as the antique chandelier glowing overhead.

The bride and groom had decided on a small wedding, and friends and family had gathered at Hillcrest House for their reception. The sprawling Victorian with its peaked turrets and dormer windows sat elegantly atop a bluff overlooking the ocean. The upper two floors had been converted into hotel rooms while the first-floor dining room was now a high-class, intimate restaurant. The ballroom had mostly remained untouched, still in use after 125 years. With its intricate mahogany wainscot, hand-carved moldings and coffered ceilings, the location added to the romance of Nick and Darcy's wedding reception.

Debbie nodded at the older woman's words. "They do," she agreed. "It was a beautiful wedding."

"Mmm-hmm. It's always a pleasure to see young people in love. Nick and Darcy, Sophia and Jake, Sam and Kara…" The mother of the groom's gaze turned speculative. "And you and Drew certainly make a good-looking couple."

Debbie should have seen it coming. This was the second wedding where she and Drew had walked down the aisle together as part of a wedding party. The matchup made perfect sense, as they were both single. What didn't make as much sense was the rush of heat to her face as she fought to squirm beneath his mother's speculative gaze. Praying her cheeks weren't as bright as the burgundy bridesmaid's dress she wore, Debbie shook her head.

"Mrs. Pirelli—"

"Now, how many times have I asked you to call me Vanessa? You know you're practically family."

"You're exactly right, Vanessa. All of your sons have always been like big brothers to me. There's never been anything romantic between any of us. Including me and Drew."

Not even the night of Darcy's bachelorette party.

In the days since, Debbie convinced herself whatever she thought had happened between her and Drew within the faint glow of her shop windows…hadn't. Drew had simply been looking out for her, same as always, his parting words a brotherly warning and not a sensual promise.

With that in mind, she'd gone out of her way to treat him the same as always. She'd met his gaze with a big smile and had taken his arm for their walk down the aisle with a friendly tug. She had *not* noticed the strength of the bicep linked with her own any more than she'd felt a shiver race across her shoulders when that muscled arm brushed against her. And she most certainly did not keep sneaking looks at him out of the corner of her eye to see if he was sneaking looks at her.

Because he wasn't, and that was that.

Vanessa sighed. "You can't blame a mother for trying to find the right girl for her son. After all, you're a beautiful, strong, confident woman."

Though the trim brunette with sparkling green eyes didn't have any resemblance to Debbie's own well-rounded, blond-haired, blue-eyed mother, the warmth and kindness of the words surrounded Debbie like one of her mother's vanilla-scented hugs. "Thank you, Vanessa. That means a lot to me."

"And, if I do say so myself, my son is not such a bad catch, either."

Tipping her head back with a laugh, Debbie couldn't help but agree, and not just because she was talking to Drew's mother. "You're absolutely right. Drew is a good man. One of the best, which makes him a wonderful friend."

But not the man for her. Drew was as grounded and stable as the houses he built. Not at all the type to rush headlong into adventure and excitement. Worse, Debbie thought as pinpricks of heat stabbed at her, he had known her for her entire life. He'd probably be able to recall every fashion disaster, every bad hair day, every extra pound that haunted her past. She wanted a man who would look at her and see her *now,* as the strong, confident woman Vanessa described and not as the chubby, awkward girl she'd once been.

Debbie glanced over her shoulder at Drew, knowing right where he was standing even while pretending not to. Her breath caught as their gazes met and held. He wasn't looking at her like he was remembering her fashion disaster/bad hair days. If she didn't know better—

A flush started at her painted toes and made a slow, sensual climb. If she didn't know better she might have thought he was looking at her the same way a dieting man always looked at her buns—her sugar-glazed cinnamon buns, that was—like he wanted to devour her and not stop until they were both satisfied. But that was crazy, wasn't it?

After all, this was *Drew* she was thinking about. Even-keel, think-things-through Drew Pirelli. He wasn't the kind of man to devour desserts. More the type to savor a meal, to take things slow and—

How exactly is this helping? she demanded of herself even as she tore her gaze away.

"Well, it's not unheard of for friendship to turn to something more," Vanessa remarked. "If you keep an open heart, you never know what might happen."

The echo of the words Drew had spoken the other night spurred Debbie into action. This was *not* happening. After asking Vanessa to excuse her, she grabbed a glass of champagne on her way across the floral-patterned carpet. If she decided to have some kind of reckless affair—and she had to admit, that was way more talk than action on her part so far—she had the right kind of man in mind. That was not Drew Pirelli.

Drew was the kind of man a woman committed to wholeheartedly and for her entire life. Debbie wasn't ready for that. Just the thought sent a suffocating panic pressing down on her chest. She was ready for fun. So no matter how great of a guy Drew was, and he was the greatest, he was her friend. And the sooner they got back on friendly terms, the…safer she would feel.

And how's that kind of thinking fit a daring woman out for reckless affair?

Ignoring the mocking voice in her head, Debbie smiled as she reached Drew's side. It was what she called her Bonnie's Best smile, the one she'd put on for her mother all those years ago to show Bonnie she could focus entirely on her own health because her daughter was doing just fine. The same smile she'd used to greet neighbors and friends when they asked about her mother's health and later when they inquired about Debbie in the weeks and months after Bonnie's death.

Doing just fine! Thanks so much for asking.

The smile had gotten her through much tougher times than a sudden and inappropriate infatuation with Drew Pirelli.

Pointing her champagne flute at him, Debbie spoke before Drew had the chance. "I have a bone to pick with you!" Her smile felt a little less forced as she went on the offensive. The teasing, confrontational tone was just right for their relationship. It was as comfortable and familiar as Drew himself, and only their surroundings at the posh hotel ballroom kept her from giving a lighthearted pop on the shoulder. "You cost me fifty bucks."

His dark brows rose, and he met her mock anger with a smile. But was there something different there? Something other than his usual, almost patronizing expression? He waited, biding his time, until she reached his side. His breath teased the bare skin of her neck as he leaned close and asked, "How did I do that?"

Debbie fought off a shiver threatening to shake her down to her shoes. "The bet, remember? I thought for sure you would be the next Pirelli to fall and yet Sam's already engaged. How the heck did that happen?"

He frowned as if seriously weighing her words. "Maybe you don't know me as well as you think you do."

His espresso eyes challenged her, and Debbie's confidence started to tremble right along with her suddenly weak knees. Swallowing, she countered, "More like I don't know *Sam.* After all, he's the one who got engaged when I never thought he would."

"And *I'm* the one who's still single. Maybe I'm not as settled as you seem to think."

If anyone was *unsettled,* Debbie decided, it was definitely her. She should walk away now, while she still could, while she still had any hope of getting back on equal footing with Drew again. But that was ridiculous because she did know him. She knew him well enough to realize he was messing with her, giving her a hard time, same as always. *She* was the one who was overreacting thanks to her foolish decision to give voice to her fantasies. She was the one who'd let the crazy thoughts out, and it was going to be up to her to put them back where they belonged.

"Come on, Drew. Tell me you don't see yourself married with a couple of kids." A look of admission flashed in his eyes, and Debbie pressed her point. Nodding in Nick and Darcy's direction, she said, "Tell me you don't want that."

He glanced over at the happy couple, who were busy staring into each other's eyes. "Sure, I do," he agreed readily enough for Debbie to think she'd been right all along about him playing her. "Someday. But there's something else I want right now."

She didn't realize what Drew meant until he took the slim flute from her, set it aside on a nearby table and pulled her onto the dance floor. Her hand rose automatically to rest on his shoulder and her feet quickly found the rhythm of the slow, romantic ballad. It was hardly the first time she and Drew had danced together, and as he pulled her closer, she caught scent of his cologne. The woody fragrance with its hint of cedar was the same brand he'd worn for years—a yearly Christmas gift from his sister. Sophia knew her brother wouldn't bother to buy something he'd consider unnecessary. Debbie knew it, too. She knew Drew. He was as comforting and familiar as the smell of his cologne, except—

The trip in her pulse as he spun her beneath the crystal chandelier wasn't the slow, steady pace of comfort, and she found no familiarity in the tingle of goose bumps chasing across her chest when her breasts brushed the starched front of Drew's tuxedo shirt. His eyes darkened—whether as a result of the intimate contact or in reaction to her own, Debbie didn't know, but there was no denying the heat in his gaze.

The rush of unexpected and unwanted desire took Debbie back to her teenage years and her helpless, overwhelming crush on Drew. To the unrequited longing mixed with the heartbreaking knowledge that he would never see her as anything more than his kid sister's friend. A part of her, that small part that had never lost hope even in the most hopeless of situations, longed to believe everything she was seeing in Drew's expression, longed to believe that maybe, just maybe, he did view her as more than the girl next door.

A decade-old memory drifted through her thoughts. The door to the bakery had been open, letting in the warm summer air and allowing the scents of fresh-baked breads and muffins to drift out onto the sidewalk, to lure tourists and locals inside. Standing behind the counter, she'd caught sight of Drew through the front window. He'd been away at college, but her pulse had taken that same familiar leap as if he'd never been gone a day. He'd smiled at her as he'd stepped inside and the warmth in his gaze had threatened to reach inside and pull her heart straight from her chest.

She'd cut her hair since she'd seen him last, straightening the life out of the curls she hated and taming the locks into a more sophisticated style. She'd been on yet another diet and had dropped to a smaller size. Was this the day when Drew would finally see her for who she really was? Anticipation hammered through her veins until she'd caught sight of the tall, leggy brunette on Drew's arm.

Debbie had kept her smile firmly in place as he introduced her to the girlfriend he'd met at school. She asked all the appropriate questions, showed just the right amount of friendly interest until the moment the couple said goodbye. As the two of them walked out of the shop, Debbie had heard the other girl teasingly ask if she was one of Drew's ex-girlfriends.

Nah, that's just Debbie.

She could still feel the ache of a broken heart as her dreams of Drew being her boyfriend slipped from her fingers and into the gorgeous brunette's hands. But she'd wised up after that, too, forcing herself to get over her pointless crush. She didn't want to be "just Debbie," and she refused to follow the vain hope that Drew might see her any other way.

Lifting her chin, she met his gaze head on. "If this is wedding fever, you should know I'm immune."

"Wedding fever?"

"You know," she answered. "Sympathy pains brought on by too much contact with the crazy-in-love bride and groom."

"I wouldn't call anything I'm feeling right now pain."

Debbie stumbled slightly at his words only to have Drew pull her even tighter against his chest. How many times had she dreamed of a moment like this? A moment when Drew would hold her close and finally, finally claim her mouth with his own? If he kissed her now—

Oh, if he did, Debbie had no doubt she'd fall for him all over again, wrapping herself in foolish hopes and dreams that had no place in the real world. Gazing up into his eyes beneath the chandelier's glittering lights, the promise of the longed for kiss made the risk almost, *almost* seem worth it….

Fortunately, the song came to an end, giving her the excuse to step back and take a sanity-saving breath. "That's the fever talking. You're delirious, but don't worry, it won't last."

"Debbie—"

"I need to check if Darcy needs anything. Bridesmaid's duty and all."

Quickly slipping away, Debbie ducked between the guests gathered along the edges of the dance floor, but she didn't stop to look for the bride amid the crowd. She escaped through the first doorway she found. The sound of music and laughter faded as she stepped out onto a secluded balcony overlooking the historic bed-and-breakfast's manicured grounds. The cool, ocean-scented night air touched her warm cheeks, and as Debbie gazed up at the night sky, she couldn't help thinking all the stars she'd wished upon for all those years were laughing down at her now.

As her mother had often warned her… "Be careful what you wish for," she whispered.

Drew quickly lost sight of Debbie as she darted out the French doors at the back of the ballroom. Forcing himself to let her go, he headed over to the bar and ordered a beer. He clenched the cold bottle in his hand and took a long swallow of the malty brew. She had every reason to run away from him, and he had no right to go after her until he figured out what the hell was going on.

Was Debbie right? Was he suffering from some kind of wedding fever? The explanation made as much sense as anything he could come up with to justify why he was suddenly tempted to throw caution aside when he was with her. Which was crazy, since reason had always trumped emotion in every hand he'd ever played. His head always ruled his heart. How many times had his last girlfriend, Angie, told him to stop thinking and start feeling whenever the inevitable "where is this relationship going?" talk came up?

He'd tried telling her how he felt—he found her attractive, he enjoyed spending time with her, their common interests made a good foundation for a relationship—but none of those explanations satisfied her. She'd wanted something more…just like Debbie did.

He'd overheard the words from her himself. Debbie wanted adventure, excitement, mystery—not a guy she'd known her whole life.

You're as grounded as a man can be and still manage to move both feet.

The memory of the accusation she'd made at his sister's wedding grated on his nerves, and he didn't even know why. The truth was, he prided himself on making solid decisions, on not rushing into situations without being able to predict the outcome. If he crossed the line from friendship to something more with Debbie, he had no idea where that might lead.

Yet knowing all that hadn't stopped him from asking her to dance, or from wanting more than a dance.…

She was right about one thing. If their names ended up

linked by the local grapevine, assumptions would immediately be made.

Drew snorted. With the rate his siblings were getting hitched, his parents would be sending out wedding invitations within a week.

He hadn't missed the little conversation between his mother and Debbie earlier. He could only hope his mother had been a little more subtle than she'd been after the rehearsal dinner a few nights before. A dinner he'd attended alone. He'd made excuses about work and the custom house he was building keeping him too busy for a relationship, but his mother had quickly called him out on it.

"Do you think I haven't noticed how many family dinners you've missed recently?" she'd demanded. And then softer, she questioned, "And do you think I don't know the real reason why?"

Okay, so maybe he had been feeling like the odd man out, but he wasn't about to admit that to his mother. "I've been busy. That's the *only* reason."

His mother sighed, giving him the look that could still make him feel like he was six years old. "I have to say, I never thought you would be the child I would have to worry about."

Drew winced in memory.

His mother would love nothing more than to see him settle down.

All the more reason *not* to follow Debbie out onto the secluded balcony. He almost had himself convinced when he spotted her shawl draped across the back of the chair she'd abandoned. Leaving the half-finished bottle of beer at the bar, he crossed the room to the table that had been reserved for the wedding party. And just as he'd been unable to stop himself from pulling her onto the dance floor, he reached for the softly woven shawl. The scent of her perfume, a mix of spicy and sweet that perfectly captured Debbie's personality, drifted over him. Pulling him in when he knew he should be walking away.

As he moved toward the balcony doors, he was stopped several times along the way by friends and neighbors. He took their ribbing about being the only unattached Pirelli with good humor even if the phrase "last man standing" was already getting old. He knew it would get worse after Sam's wedding. Still, he pushed the thought aside. He was a man on a mission, out to find a certain bridesmaid.

She turned as he opened the door, her arms crossed tightly to ward off the night air. For Drew, the chill was a relief after the ballroom's crowded interior. But it wasn't exactly a cold shower, and not nearly cold enough to keep his body from heating when he noticed the swell of flesh above her dress's neckline.

All brides were supposed to be beautiful, and Darcy was undeniably gorgeous. But it was Debbie who had knocked the breath from Drew's lungs when he'd caught sight of her walking down the aisle.

He should have been better prepared, seeing her now, but maybe he hadn't recovered from that first blow. Her blond hair was caught to one side, her golden curls tumbling over her shoulder. The bridesmaids' gowns reflected Darcy's taste, and Debbie looked amazing in the halter-style burgundy dress. Tiny beads highlighted the bodice, and the rich fabric fell to the tops of her strappy sandals with a slit in the side guaranteed to blow his mind with revealing flashes of her shapely calf and thigh.

Her blue eyes gazed at him warily. "Drew..."

He heard the protest in her voice and held up the shawl. "I thought you might be cold out here."

"Oh."

Was it his imagination or did she sound disappointed that he'd followed her for such an innocent reason? "Well, thank you," she said as she reached for the pink material, "but I can take care of myself."

Drew didn't doubt it. Debbie had been on her own since her mother died. Before that, really, with the care Bonnie Mattson had needed during her illness. He'd long admired Debbie's independence and the way she'd scoffed at the idea of needing a man. But for the first time, that toughness seemed to soften something inside his chest. He held on to the shawl, keeping their hands tangled together in the wispy fabric. "I know you can. But once in a while, it's nice to have someone take care of you."

Sliding the shawl from her hands, he draped the material over her shoulders, keeping hold of both ends. "Maybe," she conceded, though her slightly stiff posture wasn't giving an inch. "But I don't need—"

"This isn't about need," he interrupted. "It's about want."

Debbie swallowed. "Want?"

"It's like…dessert. Not something you need, but certainly something you crave."

"And let me guess. You're craving something *sweet*." The sardonic twist on the word told Drew what Debbie thought of that description—one he'd been guilty of using in the past. She'd nailed it when she complained to Darcy and her fellow bridesmaids about the local guys treating her like a little sister or a platonic buddy.

Standing so close to her now, feeling the heat from her body and breathing in the vanilla-and-spice scent of her skin, he wondered how the male population—himself included—could have been so deaf, blind and stupid. He had no doubt Debbie would taste sweet and yet— Suddenly he thought of the sheer temptation of her chocolate-raspberry cake. "I was thinking more along the lines of something rich, decadent, a little sinful even."

Debbie's eyes widened, huge and sparkling in the faint light streaming through the French doors. He'd gone too far, he thought. Pushed too hard for something he shouldn't even let himself want. The smart thing, the logical thing to do was to walk away now while they still could. "Debbie—"

"Seriously, Drew, has anyone ever told you that you talk too much?"

"Uh—" Before he had a chance to say anything else, she reached up, clasped her hands behind his neck and pulled his head toward hers. At the first touch of her lips, Drew was lost. Walk away? How could he when a single kiss had knocked him off his feet?

He'd been right about the sweetness, but had seriously underestimated just how rich, just how decadent she would taste, with just a hint of champagne and the piña colada wedding cake she'd made flavoring the kiss. The combination was addictive, but it was a taste uniquely her own. His tongue hungrily traced her full upper lip from corner to corner, spending an extra second at the enticing peak in the center. Diving deeper when she made a soft, indistinct sound that still managed to convey the intoxicating blend of demand and desire.

Drew might have smiled at the demand—Debbie had never been shy when it came to speaking her mind—but the desire overrode all else. He pulled her closer, her softness and curves melding against his body in a perfect fit. Blood pounded through his veins, and his hands tightened on her hips. The thin, slippery material of her dress hardly seemed like much of a barrier. With a few deft moves to push it out of the way—

The thought had barely crossed his mind when he froze

at the sound of voices drifting over from the parking lot on the other side of the evergreen hedge. The night chill seeped in as Debbie broke the kiss and slipped from his arms.

"You sure about this? Your brother is going to kill you for messing with his ride."

"I know. Great, isn't it?"

"You know what they say about payback, and your wedding is less than two months away."

Drew immediately recognized Sam's voice along with his friend Billy Cummings's. The three of them were supposed to decorate Nick's truck. Even though the newlyweds were spending their first night together at the bed-and-breakfast, their vehicle would proudly announce their just-married status for the trip home. Sam had gathered the appropriate mix of tin cans and shaving cream along with some leashes and dog toys as an homage to Nick's profession.

It wouldn't be long before—

"So where is Drew anyway? Are we doing this without him?"

"No way! He has to be part of this so I can tell Nick it was all his idea." The faint crunch of gravel followed Sam's words. "You go get the stuff, and I'll track him down."

Nick might have been the veterinarian, but Sam could be like a dog with a bone. He wasn't going to give up until he found Drew.

His looked over at Debbie, who'd already taken a few steps back. Her arms were once again crossed over her chest, but Drew didn't think this time was because of the cold. "Debbie, I'm sorry. I— That was—"

The awkwardness of the moment grew in rhythm with the silence as he tried to put the kiss and the past few minutes into words. But she clearly had her own ideas about what had taken place. "Wedding fever," she stated flatly. "But don't worry. You'll forget all about it by morning."

Then she turned and went back into the reception, leaving him alone on the balcony.

Chapter Three

Debbie took one look at the bold black letters on the whiteboard in front of The High Tide restaurant and immediately wanted to turn around and make the forty-minute drive back home from Redfield.

Singles' Night—Meet and Greet!

Nerves somersaulted through her stomach, whirling fast enough to make her feel sick. This was what she got for opening her big mouth in front of her friends. Ever since making that silly claim about wanting someone to sweep her off her feet, Sophia and Kara had been bombarding her—in person and via phone calls and emails—with ways to meet Mr. Tall, Dark and Handsome.

She'd escaped a three-way tag team only because Darcy was in Paris on her honeymoon with Nick. Though if her friend did come across any possibilities, Debbie wouldn't be surprised to receive a message touting Monsieur Tall, Dark and Handsome.

Sophia had been the one to send her the info on the singles' night. Debbie wondered what her friend would think of the sign—one she was sure normally listed the catch of the day. As if she could just order up the perfect guy to go.

Not that she was looking for the perfect guy. But she'd told Sophia she'd give it a try. She had nothing to lose, right?

Memories of the moonlit balcony swarmed her senses— the brush of Drew's lips, the subtle hint of champagne, the murmur of her name spoken against her skin. Okay, maybe she'd caught him off guard, kissing him the way she had, but he'd done a heck of a job kissing her back. It had been enough to make Debbie think that maybe he was right. Maybe she didn't know him as well as she'd always thought. Then he'd deepened the kiss, and she'd stopped thinking at all....

Debbie slammed that mental door shut. As far as she was concerned, those were all reasons *to* go to the singles' night. Drew had gotten caught up in the moment only to immediately regret it. She knew it by the what-the-hell-am-I-doing-kissing-her look in his dark gaze and the apology that had followed. And in his total absence over the past week. Not that they normally saw each other every day, but it was a small town. You couldn't avoid running into someone unless you were avoiding running into someone.

Not that she *expected* him to seek her out, but that he *hadn't*... Well, it only showed that she was right. Temporary insanity brought on by wedding fever and nothing more.

So, fine. She wasn't interested in Drew anyway. She wanted adventure, excitement. She wanted to meet someone new, and she was going to check out the daily specials on offer tonight at The High Tide.

Breathing in a deep, hopeful breath, Debbie climbed from the car and headed toward the restaurant. Redfield also catered to the tourist crowd, and the restaurant had a quaint bait-and-tackle-shop vibe—weathered wood exterior, netting and fishing rods hanging below the sign.

The scent of fried seafood was enough to make her stomach grumble even as she mentally calculated the number of calories. And while she wasn't positive her willpower would persevere, it was a sure bet that her fashion sense would win hands down.

The waistband on her floral skirt didn't have nearly enough give for her to even think about fish and chips. She'd be lucky to squeeze in a salad, but the fitted skirt was the perfect match for her favorite pale pink cashmere sweater. The purchase had been a splurge even on sale, but the savvy saleswoman had told her she looked like a cross between Marilyn Monroe and Jayne Mansfield in the figure-hugging, sinfully soft top, and Debbie had been sold.

You can do this. Sophia's voice echoed in her mind. *Just think, tonight you might meet your own Prince Charming!*

Debbie hadn't tried to explain, again, that she wasn't interested in some love of a lifetime. A relationship would only be another commitment when most days she already felt stretched too thin. Another responsibility when she already longed for more freedom. Another potential for loss when fate had already stolen so much....

But she couldn't expect Sophia, still basking in the glow of her own happily ever after, to understand that. So she'd agreed that yes, tonight might be the night.

As she stepped inside the restaurant, Debbie wondered if she hadn't underestimated the possibilities. She'd feared everyone who would go to such lengths to meet someone—herself included—would reek of desperation. But the good-looking guy standing at the bottom of the steps leading up to the reserved section of the bar met her gaze with a friendly and confident smile. He shifted the clipboard he was casually holding and held out his right hand.

"Welcome to The High Tide. Are you here for the meet and greet?" His green eyes sparkled beneath shaggy blond hair, and deep dimples bracketed his smile.

Definitely cute, and while the touch of his hand against hers didn't set off any fireworks, his grip was strong and warm. Maybe tonight could be the beginning of something after all.

"I am," she agreed, hoping she didn't sound too eager.

After taking her name and email to keep her up to date with future events, he said, "Here's a badge. We'd like you to write your name and an interesting or fun fact about yourself on it."

Debbie reached out but her gaze locked on his hand. His left hand and the shiny gold band on the fourth finger. "You're married?" she blurted out, the words escaping before she had time to call them back.

He glanced down at his wedding ring and flushed slightly. "Oh, yeah. I'm, um, not part of the singles' group," he explained. "I manage the restaurant and like to be here to make sure everything runs smoothly when we have events like this. Sorry if I—"

She waved his words aside. "No need to apologize." After all, it wasn't like he'd kissed her or anything. Withholding a sigh, she asked, "I don't suppose you and your wife met at one of these events, did you?"

His eyes lit in memory. "No, we met while backpacking along the California coastline. We were supposed to travel all the way up to Canada and at the end of the trip go our separate ways. But we realized we'd fallen in love and decided to stay together. Just goes to show that you can find love anywhere along the way. Good luck tonight."

Backpacking across the country. Now, that was a fun

and interesting fact, Debbie thought as she filled out her name badge. She got the first part done okay, but then came to a complete halt. The whole point of going to an event like this was to break out of a rut. She'd lived in the same town, in the same apartment, worked the same job and had known the same people her whole life. If her world was filled with fun and interesting facts, she doubted she'd *be* at a singles' event. No, she'd be backpacking along the coast or jetting off to Paris....

Sighing, she glanced over to the other side of the bar. She'd be sitting across the table from a good-looking guy who looked a lot like— Who looked exactly like— Oh, good grief, it *was* Drew Pirelli!

Sitting in a secluded booth, Drew and a beautiful brunette were engaged in an intense conversation, their heads bent so close together the table between them almost disappeared. As she watched, he reached over and stroked the woman's arm, and a layer of goose bumps rose along her own skin....

Abruptly turning away, Debbie nearly crumpled the name tag in her hand. She had to leave now before he saw her and— And what exactly? Who cared if he saw her out tonight?

She wasn't going to sit at home, waiting for Prince Charming to sweep her off her feet. She was taking charge and going after what she wanted. She wanted to go out, to escape the pressure of duty and responsibility for once in her life. She wanted some fun and interesting facts to write down on her stupid name badge!

Picking up the pen, she printed a few words beneath her name, capping them off with an exclamation point before slapping the sticky tag to the front of her sweater. Now, time to actually meet a single guy at this singles' event.

Within minutes, she'd done just that. Gary Tronston

was in his early thirties by her guess. He had blond hair and wore wire-framed glasses. He was a dentist, and while Debbie wasn't sure how interesting that fact was, he had added on his name tag that he was a dentist with a sweet tooth, which at least showed an attempt at a sense of humor.

But talking to him, Debbie couldn't help feeling he'd somehow slipped her a shot of Novocain.

"I like helping people. Seeing them smile," he added with a smile of his own. "It's not saving the world, but I like to think I've made a difference."

"That's great, Gary. Really."

Debbie might not have always been the best judge of men, but he seemed like a nice guy. If only she felt even the slightest spark…

She didn't, though, and it was all Drew's fault. No matter how hard she tried, she couldn't keep from glancing over poor Gary's shoulder at Drew on the other side of the bar.

His dark hair gleamed even in the bar's muted lighting, and the red T-shirt he wore, the long sleeves pushed back to reveal his tanned, muscular arms, was the perfect contrast. His eyebrows were pulled together in a frown, and though she was too far away, she knew just how rich and warm his eyes were. After a moment, his features relaxed, the lines around his eyes crinkling slightly as he flashed his perfect white teeth in a smile at his date. Debbie tore her gaze away, but it was too late. He looked so vibrant, so virile, that Gary with his blond hair and somewhat pasty skin seemed ready to simply fade away.

Not that Gary was to blame. When she and Drew had kissed, the whole world had faded away. How was the poor guy supposed to compete with that?

"Would you like a drink?" he asked before waving their waitress over and requesting a wine list as if they were at a five-star establishment instead of a casual, family-friendly restaurant. She tried to ignore that it made him seem more than a little pretentious. But once she spotted that chink in his armor, she couldn't help noticing a few more less than attractive details. Like when he mentioned for the third time that he drove a Mercedes. And that he'd graduated with honors. And that he was working with a group of investors to build an exclusive resort in the area.

Debbie supposed it would have been hard to fit all that on a name tag.

Suppressing a sigh, she smiled as the waitress returned with their drinks and took a sip of the white wine Gary had ordered for both of them. She fought to keep her attention on the man in front of her instead of on the one across the bar. But that focus only brought more details to light. Like…wasn't Gary's blond hair combed a little too neatly? His clothes too perfectly pressed? And she'd bet the bakery that the shine on his nails came from a manicure.

Good hygiene was one thing, but that was just…weird, she decided, reaching for her wineglass again. Drew would never—

Debbie tried to stop the hopeless comparison, but suddenly the floodgates were open. There was nothing overstated about Drew, nothing that said he was trying too hard or that he was too hung up on his own good looks. Just a quiet confidence and yes, he was gorgeous enough for Debbie to be hung up on his looks. Of course, he was more than a pretty face and a drool-worthy bod.

He was…Drew.

The boy who'd stood up for her when some of the other kids in school had teased her about her weight and the outrageous desserts her mother always packed in her lunch. Of course, he'd been thirteen at the time and helped her in typical boy fashion—by stealing huge bites out of her cupcake or éclair or torte when Debbie wasn't watching and then flashing her a cocky grin. In typical girl fashion, Debbie had protested, calling him names and probably sticking her tongue out a time or two, even as warmth bloomed inside her.

At nine years old, she'd known he was saving her from pigging out in front of the rest of the class or from hurting Bonnie's feelings by refusing to take those desserts to school or, heaven forbid, throwing out the food her talented mother made with such love.

And then there was the day of her mother's funeral. Just about everyone in town had stopped by to tell her how much her mother would be missed and how they would be there for Debbie if she needed anything.

She'd smiled through it all, reminiscing about her mother, talking about how much she loved to bake and to share her gift of sweets with the town. Only later did Debbie break down in the back of the bakery, crying over a batch of éclairs that she had never, ever been able to make as well as Bonnie, as it hit her that she would never taste her mother's baking again. It was then, after everyone else was gone and she was alone, that Drew knocked on the bakery's back door. He hadn't said much, simply holding her as she cried and then helped her to clean up the mess she'd made of the kitchen.

He'd told her everything would be okay, and though countless others had offered that same platitude, wrapped in Drew's arms, breathing in the familiar scent of his aftershave and listening to the quiet confidence in his deep voice, she'd believed him. And she'd held on to that belief deep in her heart, pulling it out when life got rough and she'd had her doubts about running the business on her own or during the holidays when at times she felt so alone. And somehow she knew everything would be all right. Because Drew had told her so, and he would never go back on his word.

This time, she couldn't keep her glance from straying over toward his booth. Her heart slammed against her rib cage when his dark-eyed gaze snared hers. His date had disappeared, and he was looking back at her without a hint of surprise. A wash of heat crept up her face. How long had he been watching her while she'd been trying so hard not to watch him? And was he really going to sit there the rest of the night, studying her as she pretended to have a good time? Because, yes, by now she was past the point of convincing herself she actually *was* having a good time.

She reached for her glass, surprised to find it almost empty, but thankfully the waitress quickly stopped by with reinforcements. She started when Gary reached out and grabbed her hand. "I'm so glad you came to this event. It's hard to meet the right person, isn't it?"

The right person? Oh, good Lord, she really hoped he wasn't talking about her! "Um, yeah. Look, Gary—"

"I knew as soon as I saw you that you were the one."

Debbie swallowed. "Gary, that's so…sweet of you to say. But the thing is…" Oh, jeez. She hated doing this. She'd been on the other side of the "it's not you, it's me" speech too many times not to feel badly about delivering it. "I'm not really looking for anything serious. I just want to meet some new people, to go out and have a good time."

His sincere expression quickly morphed into one that was far more interested. "Well, in that case, why don't we get out of here? I've booked a room in a hotel just down the street where we can really have some fun."

"Whoa, there, Gar! I think you still have the wrong idea about me. But, you know, good luck with all that!"

Grabbing her glass, Debbie downed half the wine in a single gulp as she made her escape.

Speaking of which... Yep, Drew was still in the corner booth. Still watching...which meant as much as tonight was starting to look like a bust, she couldn't go home yet. She didn't want to give Drew the satisfaction of thinking that he'd run her off or worse, that he was right and that she should be spending her nights at home alone like a good girl.

She was going to have fun tonight, she thought grimly, even if it killed her.

She was killing him.

Drew's hand tightened around the soda he'd been downing all night. He hadn't come to the bar to drink, though that was the invitation he'd issued to Cassidy Carter. It had been strictly business, and he didn't drink on the job. Of course, Cass had left over an hour ago, and he still hadn't switched to anything harder than pure sugar and caffeine. He was a little afraid of what he might do if even so much as a beer went to his head. Hell, the rate the night was going, he should probably switch to diet and caffeine-free.

Every time Debbie laughed, every time she touched another guy—even if it was just to shake hands—every time she leaned closer to hear what one of them said, every damn time the guy's gaze dropped to the rounded curves on display beneath a sweater that looked like it was made out of cotton candy, Drew had to fight to keep his butt in the booth.

He'd always considered himself a patient man, but he was quickly running out. Still, he kept waiting. Waiting for Debbie to realize none of these losers were good enough for her. He could see it at first glance. What was taking her so damn long?

He'd thought overhearing Debbie at Darcy's bachelor-ette party was bad. But that had only been words, and he'd done his best to convince himself it was just talk. That she wasn't serious about wanting some stranger to sweep her off her feet. Clearly, he was wrong. Not only had Debbie meant every word, she was backing them up with actions.

And it was killing him.

Drew didn't want to look too closely at the reasons why. Debbie was an old family friend, and he was worried about her. That was reason enough, right? He didn't want to think that he was jealous or that he wanted to be one of the men standing close enough to her to know if that sweater could possibly feel as soft as it looked. He certainly didn't want to think about any of those men kissing her the way he had on the balcony last weekend because he shouldn't have been the one kissing her, either. Tonight only drove that home more than ever. How could he be the one to protect her if he had to worry about protecting her from himself?

But when the waitress brought Debbie yet another glass of wine and when the introduction handshakes turned into nice-to-meet-you hugs, he couldn't stand by any longer.

He was saving her from herself. When she came to her senses and forgot all about this whole adventure and excitement streak she was on, she'd realize that, too. She'd probably even thank him for it.

A burst of mocking laughter that sounded just like his brothers' echoed in his head.

Yeah, sure she would.

Debbie wasn't sure how long she'd been talking to the brown-haired guy standing in front of her before she realized she no longer held his full attention. His gaze kept flicking toward a point over her shoulder. She might have feared she was too boring to hold his interest, but boredom didn't put a look of fear in a guy's eyes.

"I think I should, um…" He was already backing away before he blurted out, "Nice meeting you, Debbie."

She didn't have to turn around to around to know Drew was behind her. "What are you doing, Drew?" she asked as she drained the last of her wine and motioned to the waitress for another glass.

"I was going to ask you the same thing."

"I am here for singles' night." She turned to face him, feeling herself wobble slightly in her new shoes. She should have gone with the boots instead of the heels, but the pumps had the cutest bow on the toe…. "And you should be with your date."

A frown pulled his dark brows together. "I'm not on a date."

"I'm pretty sure I didn't imagine the brunette you were with earlier."

"That wasn't a date. She's a coworker on a custom house I'm building in the area."

"You always hold hands with your coworkers? I bet your subcontractors love that."

"We weren't holding hands. Cassidy was upset and I was trying to reassure her. The client we're working for is a real nightmare, and Cass is ready to quit. None of which explains what you're doing here."

"I told you. It's singles' night, and I'm single," she said, crossing her arms and meeting his scowl with a smirk.

He mimicked her actions, minus the smirk, folding his muscular arms over his broad chest, as he replied, "Well, so am I."

"You're not signed up for this event," she protested.

Glancing over at a nearby high-top table, he spotted the clipboard and a few leftover name tags. Within seconds, he'd scrawled his name across the sign-in sheet and slapped a tag to his broad chest. His name in bold, block letters with the word *contractor* written beneath. "It's not supposed to be a business card, Drew," she said as she reached out and poked him right in the name tag.

He caught her hand and held it for a moment as his gaze dropped to her chest. Or at least to the name badge on her sweater. "Obviously."

Debbie blinked, for a second having forgotten what she'd written on her own tag. "Oh, yeah. That."

Hungry for the taste of adventure....

It had sounded like something fun to write down at the time, so why did she suddenly feel embarrassed, like a teenager caught by her mother making out with a boy on the front porch? She didn't know. She couldn't even be sure how a moment like that would have felt. She'd never dated as a teenager. She'd never had the opportunity to do so many things.

And that was why she was willing to take a chance on this singles' group. Okay, so tonight had been a bit of a disappointment. There were other events planned. This night was only the beginning. She smiled her thanks and handed the waitress some cash in exchange for another glass of wine.

Lifting her chin, she met Drew's gaze head on. "You're not my big brother, Drew. I don't need you to rescue me."

A flash of guilt flickered across his expression, and Debbie realized she'd nailed it. He really did think of her like a little sister, someone to look out for, someone to protect. She took a swallow of wine to wash away the ache in her throat. So much for thinking he might have been jealous. So much for the foolish hope that he'd approached her because he wanted to be the guy she was talking to instead of the half a dozen or so men whose names she'd already forgotten.

Catching her by the wrist, he took the wineglass from her hand and set it aside. "I think you've had enough."

"You've got that right," she muttered. She'd certainly had enough of him!

Pushing past him, she headed for the exit. The cool, quiet night air brushed her heated cheeks, a welcome relief from the noisy, crowded restaurant. Her heels crunched unevenly across the asphalt, but she didn't get far before he caught up with her again.

"You shouldn't be driving."

"I didn't have that much to drink."

"You had four glasses of wine."

"You were counting?" Debbie snorted, only to realize maybe that was a good thing since she seemed to have stopped keeping track after two. No wonder the asphalt was rocking beneath her feet, and the stars were shooting like a pretty kaleidoscope overhead....

"Let me take you home."

Oh, why did Drew's murmured words have to sound so much better than any of the invitations she'd heard from potential dates that evening? Not that he meant anything by it. Just like he hadn't meant anything by the kiss they'd shared. "You can't fool me."

He was playing the role of the white knight—offering rides home and apologizing for kisses when he should have been kissing her again.

"What?"

"What, what?" She hadn't said anything. Oh, crap, what had she said?

Frowning, Drew asked, "How is asking to give you a ride home trying to fool you?"

Relieved she hadn't spilled anything too embarrassing, yet still annoyed, she snapped, "You didn't offer to drive me home. You asked to take me home. As in, 'Let's go back to your place.' You think I don't know a come-on when I hear one, Drew Pirelli?"

Just like she knew very well when she *hadn't* heard one, but she found herself entirely unwilling to let him off the hook so easily.

"That's not— I didn't—" A pained expression crossed his face, and he ran a frustrated hand through his hair. Blowing out a breath, he started again, "Debbie, I—"

Feeling another apology coming on, she threw up a dismissing hand and started walking. Not that she would risk driving home, but she had a coat in her car and if she had to wait who knew how long for a cab, she'd rather not have to stand around shivering.

But she only made it a few steps before the ground slipped out from beneath her feet. And not because she'd fallen. Her startled gasp ended in a mousy squeak as Drew swept her up into his arms. The stars spun wildly overhead, and without thought she clung to his shoulders. Their gazes collided for a heat-filled second before his mouth crashed down on hers in a stunning kiss.

If that night on the balcony had been wedding fever, this was a different level of heat altogether. The kiss tasted of frustration and passion, a fight-fire-with-fire kind of burn that promised so much more—

The earth may well have moved, but Debbie didn't realize Drew had until he plopped her into the passenger seat of his car. His breathing still ragged from the kiss, he repeated, "You're not driving home."

Despite the way the world was still tilting around her, every ounce of independent woman roared inside her. Realizing her hands were still fisted in his shirt, she pushed him away. "I can*not* believe you just did that!"

Drew's jaw tightened as he leaned closer, until she could

catch a hint of his aftershave mixed with the woodsy night air. "Believe it."

The vehicle's dome light wasn't very bright, but in its faint glow, she saw something in his hardened expression. Something that made her pulse pound even harder. Something that made her wonder if she was seeing Drew in a different light…or if something had changed in the way he was seeing her.

And she had the feeling that as surprised as she was by his actions, he'd surprised himself even more.

Chapter Four

I cannot believe you just did that!

Debbie's outraged words rang in his head on the silent drive back home. Drew couldn't believe it himself. His hands tightened on the steering wheel as he glanced over at Debbie. She was looking out the side window, giving him little more than a view of the back of her head, but he could imagine the fire in her blue eyes. She had every right to be pissed and to give him the cold shoulder, but her silence at least allowed him the time to get his emotions back under control.

Damn if he couldn't hear Angie laughing at him now.

His former girlfriend had accused him more than once of not *having* emotions. *If I walk out this door right now, you won't even try to stop me, will you?* she'd demanded during the fight that led to their breakup. Truth was, he had tried to stop her. He'd talked about how good they were together, how much they had in common. He brought up the time they'd both invested in the relationship and asked if she really wanted to throw that away.

But even as the words were coming out of his mouth—logical, sensible words—he'd known it wasn't enough. Whatever Angie wanted, he didn't have it within himself to give it to her. And that was the reason why he hadn't stopped her when she did finally walk out that door.

Never once had it occurred to him to physically pick Angie up and kiss her to try to convince her to stay. Watching Debbie walk away…that instinct had been undeniable.

And it didn't make sense! Debbie wasn't his girlfriend. She was his friend. And while he wouldn't have let her drive home even if he hadn't known her her entire life, he could have stopped her another way. Hell, all he'd had to do was take her purse and the keys inside. Simple, easy, logical. And yet that solution had never occurred to him.

Drew shifted in the driver's seat. He didn't know what was going on, but he didn't like it. He wanted things to go back to the way they used to be when he didn't know how it felt to have Debbie's soft sweater and softer curves pressed against him. When he didn't have the memory of her kiss replaying again and again through his mind. When he didn't have to fight his imagination to keep the kiss from becoming more than a kiss as his lips moved lower to taste the curves of her breasts….

He'd stopped, or if he were totally honest with himself, he'd been interrupted, that night on the balcony before he could take things further. And yet his fingertips tingled with the thought of tracing the soft, pale skin beneath the burgundy dress she'd worn. He could hear her trembling sighs as his touch became more intimate, more arousing.

Swearing beneath his breath, he pushed the fantasy aside and focused on the headlights cutting through the darkness beyond the windshield. As the winding mountain roads gave way to the gentler slopes leading into town, he glanced over at the woman beside him. "Debbie?"

No response.

"Look, I know you're angry, but you have to understand…" His voice trailed off, at a loss to explain something he couldn't figure out for himself.

The silence from the other side of the SUV continued, and he leaned forward for a closer look. Okay, so she wasn't pissed off and ignoring him. She was sound asleep.

Drew sighed and dropped his head back. Great. Just great.

He didn't want to leave her alone like this, but he couldn't stay if he took her back to her place. Debbie lived in the apartment above the bakery right on Main Street. Someone was bound to notice his truck parked outside her shop all night.

That made his place the better choice, though he doubted Debbie would think so.

Drew lived just outside of town. The Craftsman-style homes in his neighborhood would be hitting the century mark soon, but all were well cared for with nicely maintained yards. Columns and pillars bracketed wide porches marked with front swings and whiskey barrels and hanging pots filled with mums and pansies and petunias.

He'd rented the house for the past several years, liking the consistency of knowing the people who lived around him in the established neighborhood, but he'd always known it was temporary. His dream home had existed in his mind for years, and before long it would be a reality.

Debbie hadn't stirred by the time he'd parked in the driveway and circled around to open the passenger door. The dome light glowed from behind her, illuminating her blond hair and giving her an almost angelic halo. He smiled wryly when he thought of how she might take that comparison. Why she wanted to make a break with the person she was and try to be someone else, he didn't know. Not when she was already perfect.

God, she was pretty. Her dark eyelashes fanned against her cheeks and, even without her bold and sassy smile, he could see the faint hint of the dimple that flashed every time she laughed. The smell of her sweet and spicy perfume tempted him to lean closer, to find the exact spot of ivory skin she'd touched with the scent. Whatever lipstick she'd had on earlier that night had worn away, leaving her mouth a natural pink he hadn't been able to resist.

How was it that he'd known her all her life without really knowing her at all?

She stirred suddenly as if roused by his stare—or maybe even by his earthshaking thoughts—and blinked those bright blue eyes at him. "Wake up, Sleeping Beauty," he murmured.

"Drew— What—" Her gaze focused over his shoulder. "What are we doing here?" She sat up straight, and he could see the moment all that wine went to her head. Her eyes closed again, her face paled and her throat moved as she swallowed hard.

"Are you gonna be sick?"

"If I am, you might want to step back."

Drew laughed even as he leaned closer to unhook her seat belt. She needed someone to look after her, and that was a role he felt comfortable with—even if the idea of Debbie sleeping under his roof did send a pulse of heat through his veins. "Come on. I'm not leaving you alone like this, and I've got a Pirelli family secret recipe, thanks to Sam, guaranteed to take away the worst of a hangover."

He helped her inside, figuring he could judge how poorly she was feeling by her total lack of resistance. It struck him then that Debbie had never been to his place even though she was a common fixture at family gatherings at his parents' house. Now wasn't exactly the time for a tour, not that there was much to see. The living room, with its man-cave style furnishings of oversize recliners and couch, well-worn coffee tables and wall-mounted flat-screen TV, branched off into hallways on either side. One led to the master bedroom, the other to the secondary bedrooms and guest bath.

He guided Debbie through the arched doorway to his tiny dining room. She sank into the chair he pulled out for her and sat with her head in her hands. A short peninsula countertop separated the dining nook from the rest of the kitchen, so he could easily keep an eye on her as he proceeded to fix what really amounted to watered-down hot tea mixed with some lemon and honey. The drink was ready within minutes and he carried it over to her.

She looked miserable, a far different girl from the one who'd tied his guts into knots as she laughed and flirted through the night. A very small part of him was enjoying her discomfort as payback for what she'd put him through, but at least now it was over. Certainly after tonight, she'd have learned her lesson and this would be the end of her ridiculous search for some stranger to come along and sweep her off her feet.

"Careful. It's hot," he said as he set the mug in front of her.

Okay, that warning at least earned him a glare, but she did blow on the surface of the steaming liquid before taking a sip. "Hmm, this is good. Thanks."

"You're welcome," he said as he leaned back against the counter. "As soon as you finish that, I'll get you some more comfortable clothes to change into, and you can crash in the guest room."

"You really don't have to do all this, you know." She

lifted her chin to a stubborn angle even as she laced her fingers around the warm mug—like holding on with both hands would somehow keep her steady. "I've been taking care of myself for a long time."

And she'd taken care of her mother for many years before she'd been on her own. A pinprick of guilt stabbed him. Despite his earlier thoughts, Debbie deserved to go out and have a good time. Why did it bother him so much that she wanted to? She was perfectly capable of taking care of herself. That independent streak was something she had in common with Angie. But unlike with his last girlfriend, Drew was having a hard time fighting his own protective instincts.

"I know. Your mother would be proud of you."

Looking up from the mug of tea, her eyes widened—big and blue and beautiful. Drew felt a moment's panic when they started to fill with tears. Debbie never cried. Or at least, not that he'd ever seen—except that one time.

Nearly the whole town had turned out for her mother's funeral, and everyone who attended had taken the time to speak to Debbie and offer their condolences. Drew wasn't sure what had made him slip away from the crowd or why he'd gone to the bakery later that evening. But he'd taken one look at Debbie's face and the tears she was trying so hard to hide and pulled her into his arms.

They'd never talked about that day, but he had to wonder if she could see the memory reflected in his gaze. She blinked her eyes quickly as she pushed away from the table, her movements slow and careful. "Drew…"

She reached out toward him, and time seemed to stand still. He was caught in the moment, spellbound by the intimate silence of the late night. It was as though he was standing on the brink of two worlds. The one he knew where he and Debbie always had been and always would

be friends and a new, uncertain world where anything—
anything—could happen. His blood heated at the possibilities, and when she touched him, placing her hand against
his chest, he felt as though she'd given him a violent shove.
One that had him teetering on the edge of crossing that
line between friendship and so much more....

She whispered his name again, the longing in the single
word grabbing hold of a need inside of him and refusing to
let go. He reached up, cupping her face in his hands, and
his thumb brushed against a tear. Damp and salty between
his rough, calloused skin and the softness of Debbie's. Her
eyes still had a watery cast, and he was taken back once
more to the day of the funeral. A day when he'd wrapped
Debbie in his arms to comfort her.

There'd been nothing sexual about it—one friend offering comfort to another.

But that wouldn't be the case tonight. If he crossed that
line, it may never be the case again....

Reining in the desire raging through him took every
ounce of the self-control that had deserted him earlier.
Kissing her without thinking his actions through had been
a mistake he wouldn't repeat. He wouldn't let himself rush
into this. Not when Debbie might regret the decision in
the light of day. She talked a tough game, but her guard
was down right now, revealing a vulnerability her bright
smile and smart mouth normally disguised.

Touching his lips against her forehead when he wanted
the taste, the texture, the temptation of her mouth beneath
his more than he wanted his next breath, he pulled away.
Her pale eyebrows pulled together, her confusion a contrast to the flush of arousal coloring her cheeks and paint-
ing her parted lips. "Drew, what—"

"Time for bed, princess. I'll go get those clothes." He
hurried from the kitchen, half expecting to feel the ceramic

mug crash against the back of his head. The patronizing nickname might have taken things too far, but he needed to find his footing and the familiar teasing brought him back to solid ground. And he wasn't moving from there until he'd given serious thought to the direction he was heading.

Debbie squinted against the early-morning sunlight and fought the urge to hide under the covers and sleep for a few more hours. Rolling to her side, her head spun in protest. Ugh, make that a few more days.

She tried to swallow, but her throat was so dry her tongue felt like sandpaper against the roof of her mouth. Oh, she was never going to drink again. Pushing aside the covers, she slipped out of Drew's bed. Okay, technically it was his guest bed, and you'd think if she was going to suffer the physical effects of too much alcohol that she'd at least have the mental relief of not recalling everything that happened the night before. But no, there it was—the memory rearing its ugly, embarrassing head...

Lifting a hand to touch his chest.... Seeing the look in his eyes and foolishly thinking he wanted to kiss her as badly as she wanted to him to.... The way she'd practically begged him to....

And then the touch of his lips against her forehead before he shooed her off to bed like she'd been an eight-year-old guest at one of Sophia's slumber parties.

Heat burned in her cheeks. How was she ever going to face him again?

It's never too late to leave town, she thought grimly.

But one thing was for sure, she decided as she caught a glimpse of herself in the mirror above the dresser. Her blond hair had turned corkscrew wild from all the tossing and turning the night before, and what was left of her makeup was smeared beneath her bloodshot eyes. And she was wearing his clothes—the dark blue, sinfully soft T-shirt and black drawstring shorts he'd left for her outside the bathroom where she'd taken refuge after humiliating herself in the kitchen.

She was not facing him like this.

Cracking the bedroom door, she listened for a moment. She didn't hear any sounds from the rest of the house. Biting her bottom lip, she stepped out into the hall. If she could make her escape while Drew was still sleeping, she could save at least the tiniest bit of her pride. Yes, that would mean doing the walk of shame through town to get back home since her car was still in The High Tide parking lot, but she couldn't think of anyone she'd rather see less at that moment than Drew. And, of course, it wasn't a real walk of shame since that expression was reserved for slipping away the morning after sleeping with someone and she hadn't slept with Drew…which made the whole thing…that…much…worse.

Mentally calling herself and Drew every name she could think of and longing to be in the bakery where she could bang cookie sheets and baking pans as loud as possible, she tiptoed into the bathroom where she'd left her clothes and purse the night before. She eased the door closed behind her, careful not to make even the slightest sound, then hurriedly glanced around for her things. The neatly folded pile sitting on the vanity caught her eye, and Debbie swallowed. In her best moments, she didn't fold her clothes once she'd already worn them. She certainly wouldn't have done so on a night where she was hungover and humiliated.

Reaching out, she touched the cashmere, her heart skipping a beat when she thought of Drew running his work-roughened hands over the soft fabric. But then she remembered he hadn't wanted to run his hands over *her* and she tossed the borrowed clothes aside and jerked the sweater on with far less care than the delicate material deserved.

It took some doing, but thanks to the tiny brush, compact and mini tube of lipstick she carried in her purse, she managed to look halfway decent. Now she just needed her shoes. She had a vague recollection of slipping them off as she sat at the kitchen table. Pressing her feet flat against the cool tile had been a relief after standing around in heels all night.

Another peek through the doorway confirmed Drew was nowhere in sight, and she literally tiptoed down the hall and into the kitchen. Yes! Spotting one of her beige heels beneath the table, she ducked underneath to pick it up. She was glancing around for its mate when she heard Drew's voice coming from outside.

For a split second, she froze. Good Lord, who was he talking to? She'd thought he was still sleeping, but that was definitely his voice coming from the porch. In the next moment, she heard the front door open and sprang into action. Scrambling backward, she tried standing too soon and cracked her head on the underside of the table. Her eyes stung at the sharp pain, but she ignored it as she glanced around wildly one more time for her missing shoe.

Drew spoke again, but she was in too much of a panic to pay attention to the words. There was no way she could slip by and hide out in one of the bedrooms, so she took the only escape route available.

Holding tight to her lone shoe, she ducked out the back door and onto the porch overlooking the backyard. Her pulse was pounding in her ears even as she tried to hear what was going on inside. She'd probably been fooling herself when she thought she would walk home in the early-morning mist, and she couldn't even pretend like she'd be able to make the trek barefoot. She heard Drew's voice again, and this time the words penetrated.

"Hey, Debbie?"

Her heart slammed against her chest. What was he thinking? Didn't he know what anyone would assume after finding her at his house first thing in the morning? She didn't have time to formulate any kind of excuse before the back door opened, and Drew was gazing at her in confusion from the doorway.

"What are you doing?" he asked.

"What am I doing? What are you doing?" she demanded, her voice a harsh whisper. "Why would you bring someone into the house? What if they figure out that I'm here?"

His expression cleared, a slight smile tilting his lips. "Oh, she already figured that out. She's got a really good sense of smell."

Smell? The absurdity of the conversation made Debbie question whether or not this was real. Maybe she was still asleep in her bed at home, and none of this had ever happened.

Drew stuck his head back inside the door and called out, "Come here, Rain!"

A second later, a black streak of fur darted out in a beeline for Debbie's bare toes. *This* was who Drew had been talking to? Relief and reaction to the puppy's sheer cuteness soon had a wry smile tugging at her lips. The exuberant licking tickled, and she tried not to do some ridiculous dance to escape the puppy's quick-moving tongue. She'd already made a big enough fool of herself in front of Drew this morning. Never mind her humiliating behavior the night before.

Focusing on the dog was much easier than focusing on the man standing in front of her, looking good enough to eat in faded jeans and a red sweatshirt. The early morning breeze had ruffled his dark hair and brought out a ruddiness in his cheeks. His dark eyes sparkled, and he looked awake and energized. Unlike Debbie who felt tired and rumpled and, yes, hungover.

"Dog-sitting?" she asked as she bent down to rub the puppy's silky ears. Rain gave up on Debbie's toes and jumped on her back legs, trying to reach her face with that warm, darting tongue.

"Nope," he said. "This one's all mine."

"Really?" Debbie asked as she glanced up.

She knew Darcy had taken in a stray a few months ago, unaware the dog was about to give birth. She'd called Nick, the local vet, and that had been the start of their relationship. The last Debbie had heard, Maddie, Nick's daughter, had been pushing to keep the mama dog and the four puppies, much to Nick and Darcy's dismay.

"Kara and Sam took one of the boys for Timmy," Drew said, referring to Sam's recently found four-year-old son who also happened to be Kara's nephew. "A friend of Maddie's took the other girl. I think Maddie's going to get her way, though, and they'll end up keeping the last boy. Unless you're interested?"

"Oh, no, not me!" Debbie straightened abruptly as if she expected him to try to foist the other puppy on her right that minute.

"Why not? You clearly like dogs."

"I do. What's not to like? They're cute and cuddly and loving, but they're also a lot of work."

"Yeah, but it's worth it," he said with a grin as Rain turned her attention toward him. The puppy was clearly smitten with her new owner, and not just because of her fascination with the laces on his tennis shoes. The affection was mutual as Drew picked up the squirming puppy and held her in his arms. His big palm just about covered her small back, and as he rubbed her silky fur, the puppy groaned in bliss.

Smart girl, Debbie thought, figuring she'd do the same if Drew buried his fingers in her hair.

Goose bumps rose on the back of her neck at the very thought. Debbie wished she could blame the reaction on the cool breeze and overcast fall morning, but she knew better. It was all Drew—the memory of his kiss and the unfulfilled promise of his caress the night before.

Crazy that the puppy snuggled in his arms didn't detract from that oh-so-masculine sexiness. Crazier still that it only added to it.

"So what exactly are you doing out here?"

"I heard you talking and thought you were bringing someone inside. The last thing I need is anyone thinking I spent the night with you."

His dark brows pulled together. "You did spend the night."

Heat touched her cheeks. "You know what I mean." Dropping her focus to her shoe, she said, "I couldn't find my other shoe."

His frown morphed into a sheepish expression as he said, "Yeah, um, about that…Rain's still teething, and she's been doing really well but—"

"No! Seriously?" Her shoulders slumping, Debbie clutched her sole surviving pump to her chest. "They were so cute."

And though she'd had them for months, they were brand-new. She'd been saving them for a special occasion, and wasn't it a sorry testament to her life that a few dozen or so weeks could go by without a special occasion in sight?

"Would it help to know it made a really awesome chew toy?"

"Oddly, no." She sighed.

"How about if Rain said she was sorry?" Drew held out the puppy as if prompting a five-year-old to remember her manners. Rain rolled her head toward Debbie, draping her neck over the crook of Drew's elbow. With one ear flopping over, her tongue hanging out the side of her mouth and her eyes bright and happy, she didn't look the least bit repentant. She did, however, look absolutely adorable, and any irritation Debbie might have felt disappeared. Toward the dog and toward the man holding her.

She'd been angry and hurt and humiliated when Drew had turned her away the night before, but in the clear light of day, she could see now that he'd made the right decision. Sexual chemistry aside—assuming, that was, that it wasn't just on *one* side—she and Drew were at different places in their lives. He was four years older than she was, and while that age difference was minimal, they'd taken very different paths to get where they were.

Though Drew had worked odd jobs as a teenager, he'd still had plenty of time for sports and extracurricular activities as well as parties and hanging out with his friends. He'd been one of the cool kids who'd gone to every high school dance, run for class office and had been nominated for homecoming king. He'd never been short on friends or girlfriends, and she assumed his years at college had been the same way.

He'd had his fun. He'd done all the things he wanted to do, including opening and running a successful business in his hometown. No matter what he said to the contrary, it only made sense that he would soon be looking toward the future—a wife, a family, a dog…

One down, Debbie thought as she reached out to stroke one of Rain's silky ears, *two to go.*

She was looking for fun and freedom, not extra responsibility, even if that only meant taking care of a dog. She'd accused the puppy of being a lot of work when, really, what she'd been thinking was how the little thing was such a huge commitment. A commitment Drew was clearly willing to make.

So staying friends was obviously the logical choice, even though her heart ached a little at the thought of Drew Pirelli never kissing her again. "No hard feelings, Rain. I know sometimes it can be really tough to do the right thing."

"Can I make you breakfast as part of that apology?" Drew offered. "Or do you need to get to the bakery?"

"I wasn't sure how late I'd be out last night, so I asked Kayla Walker to open up this morning."

"So…breakfast?"

"Do you even know how to cook?" Debbie asked as she followed him back into the kitchen. Vanessa Pirelli, Drew's mother, was known for her skill in the kitchen, but Debbie wasn't aware if the woman had passed those talents on to her son.

His expression was somewhat wry as he set Rain down on the kitchen floor where she scurried away, hopefully going off in search of a teething-approved dog toy. "I think I can manage frying an egg and working a toaster."

"Right. Okay, buster, move aside, and I'll show you how it's done."

"Really?"

"You think I only know how to bake?" Baking was her profession, but cooking— Cooking was her passion, one she so rarely indulged because she'd never enjoyed fixing an extravagant meal with no one to share it with.

Debbie wasn't sure what to make of Drew's expression as he stepped closer. He smelled like the outdoors—woodsy with a hint of ocean mist that rolled in every morning with the tide. Her pulse picked up its pace at the look in his dark eyes. A look that last night she'd thought meant he wanted to kiss her again. But that had been four glasses of wine talking, and this morning she had no excuse.

"I think," he murmured, "that you can do anything you want."

Her heart stumbled in her chest, and she turned toward the stove before Drew could read by the longing in her expression that what she really wanted to do was… well, *Drew*.

Chapter Five

Drew stared with a critical eye at the bare-bones structure in front of him. The early-morning chill formed a cloud as he exhaled a satisfied breath, and he took a drink from the steaming cup of coffee warming his hands. The framed house barely hinted at the layout and the details to come, but he could already see the finished product in his mind's eye. After all, he'd been designing and redesigning the plans for years.

He could picture the large foyer opening into the great room. A stone fireplace and rough-hewn mantel would be the room's centerpiece. And okay, yeah, a flat-screen TV, too. The oversize arcadia doors would offer a view to the mountains and pines beyond the property and lead the way to a redwood deck. Maybe he'd add an outdoor kitchen and built-in grill. A hot tub, too, while he was at it.

With the open floor plan, the flow led into the kitchen. A huge island took center stage with white cabinets and stainless-steel appliances all around. Smooth-as-glass black granite countertops would be a cool contrast to the warmth and character of the multicolored flagstone slate on the floors.

The rest of the house was dedicated to bedrooms—four of them. Three smaller rooms and a master suite. The master bedroom faced the same direction as the great room, and a wall of windows would take full advantage of the view. A view he looked forward to waking up to for the rest of his life.

Of all the homes he'd built over the years, Drew had to admit, this one was special. This one was his. Even though he put his heart, his soul, his sweat and sometimes even blood into every house he built, there was something about ownership, about possession, that gave him an extra sense of pride when he looked at the newly framed house. This time, when the house was complete, he wouldn't be handing the keys over to some other family. The house would be his, and the family...

Yeah, he wanted that, too.

The crunch of tires coming down the gravel lane caught his attention, and he whistled for Rain. The puppy was smart but still had a lot to learn, and Drew wasn't taking any chances. She bounded over to his side, tail wagging, a large stick clamped between her jaws. She sat and dropped her new toy at his feet, her expression bright and eager to please.

"Hey, cool stick, girl." Picking it up, he tossed it in the opposite direction of the approaching vehicle.

Drew didn't recognize the rugged SUV, but he grinned when he caught sight of the man behind the wheel. He walked over to the vehicle, Rain trotting faithfully at his side, the stick forgotten in light of a new person to love.

"Ryder, I'd heard you were moving back to town," he

said as he greeted the brown-haired man climbing from the driver's seat.

"You heard, huh?" Ryder Kincaid winced slightly as he shook Drew's hand. "Gonna take a while to get used to the whole small-town mentality again."

While Ryder was two years younger than Drew, both he and Nick had been friends with his older brother who still lived in town. Ryder had left Clearville after his senior year to attend college on a sports scholarship. Drew had heard the other man had taken a job at a prestigious construction company in San Francisco—working for his in-laws. He'd also heard that Brittany, Ryder's wife, was not moving back with him. Judging by the circles beneath the other man's eyes and the rough-around-the-edges stubble and overgrown hair, the separation had hit Ryder hard.

"So." Drew cleared his throat. "How have you been?"

Giving a short laugh beneath his breath, Ryder said, "Something tells me you've heard all about that, too."

"Sorry, man."

"You know what they say, it's for the best and time to move on."

From what Drew recalled, Ryder Kincaid and Brittany Baines had been high school sweethearts, prom king and queen their senior year, and both families had long expected them to marry. They'd been Clearville's golden couple, and Drew was aware of a subtle divide when it came to Ryder's return.

Half the town had welcomed the hometown kid back, taking his side on whatever had caused the split with Brittany. The other half, people who were still in touch with Brittany and her family, thought Ryder was clearly the one to blame.

It was part of small-town life—feeling that connection to the people around you. Oh, sure, sometimes little more than nosiness and boredom were at work, but most times the townspeople had a genuine investment in the lives of their friends and neighbors. They truly cared.

Suddenly, an image of Debbie came to mind—a common occurrence since bringing her home the other night. Her feminine scent, a combination of sugar and spice, of sweet and sexy, still lingered in his truck. And when he'd gone to change the sheets in the guest bedroom, he'd caught himself holding on to the pillow far longer than necessary, as if somehow holding on to the idea of her sleeping under his roof, in his bed—even if it was just the guest bed.

But she was his kid sister's best friend. Hell, she was *his* friend! He'd done the right thing in walking away. Even if she hadn't had too much to drink, even if he hadn't seen the vulnerability softening her blue gaze, pursuing Debbie would be like running through a minefield. Talk about causing a rift if things didn't work out! He could see it now—his sister and sisters-in-law on one side with his brothers on the other.

Or not.

Was he really so sure Nick and Sam would have his back if it meant being at odds with the women they loved? Drew wasn't sure he wanted to know the answer, but just the possibility of causing any kind of dissent in his close family should have been enough to shut down any thoughts he had of crossing the line from friendship with Debbie into…something more. Playing it safe made perfect sense, so why did he feel like he was going to regret not taking that chance for a long time to come?

Ryder gave Rain a final pat and stood. "Moving on to something new is actually why I'm here. I wanted to know if you're looking to hire on any help."

Drew had had the feeling Ryder's visit wasn't purely a

social call. "Things might have changed around here in the years since you've been gone, but not that much. There isn't exactly a need for commercial construction around here."

"Yeah, I noticed the lack of high-rises, but I'd just as soon get out of that work anyway. I'm more interested in home building." He jerked his chin toward the unfinished house. "This looks like quite the place."

"Yeah, it's a custom I'm working on." Other than family, Drew had told few people that the house he was building was his own. He didn't know why, but he wanted the house finished, or nearly so, before showing her off to the rest of the town. And he wanted to finish it on his own. "Ryder—"

Seeming to hear the apology Drew was about to deliver, the other man interrupted. "Or I can take on remodeling jobs that come your way. I've had a ton of experience. I put myself through college working as a handyman."

"But that's something you could do on your own. Start your own business, be your own boss," Drew suggested.

"Yeah, I'd like that. Someday. But until the divorce goes through…" Ryder shrugged, but the tension he carried in his shoulders made the effort look as easy as lifting the weight of the world. Starting up a new business while in the middle of splitting assets probably wasn't the best idea. "For now, I'm just looking for a job."

In the early years of his business, Drew had started with remodeling projects. Soon his focus had changed toward building custom homes, and as that side of the business began to take off the smaller jobs had fallen to the wayside. But with the number of old houses and businesses around town, homeowners were always needing repairs and upgrades on the turn-of-the-century Craftsman-style and even older Queen Anne and Victorian homes.

"If we put the word out," Drew said, "I bet it won't be

long before we have some clients looking for remodeling estimates."

"I can begin right away," Ryder said, a little light sparking in his tired eyes. "I'm looking for a fresh start, and this could be just the thing. I can send you references from San Francisco and my resume."

"Email them to me when you get a chance," Drew said.

The two men talked a little more about the jobs Drew was currently working on and his plans for the future before Ryder left. If things worked out, the other man would have plenty of projects to keep him busy and he might also take some of the work off Drew's shoulders.

A sense of anticipation filled him. Maybe he could move up his time frame for completing the house. He'd felt stuck in such a holding pattern lately. Maybe finishing it would give him the push to start moving forward, even if he wasn't entirely sure what he was moving toward.

You're as grounded as a man can be and still manage to move both feet.

Was Debbie right? Was the restlessness he felt not a symptom of the slow process of building his dream home to his standard of perfection but of being stuck in a rut in his personal life?

She'd told him with dead certainty that he wasn't the man for her. That he was too settled, too staid, too boring. Okay, maybe she hadn't spelled it out that baldly, but it was how she thought of him. One of the guys she'd known her whole life who could never challenge or surprise her.

The desire to prove himself to Debbie—hell, maybe even to himself—made no sense, especially not on the heels of his conversation with Ryder and his awareness of the ripple effect of a broken relationship in their close-knit town.

"Come on, Rain. Time to get to work." The puppy

barked in response to her name and bounded over to his side, her tail wagging for all she was worth.

One good thing about being the boss—it meant making the rules, and as of a few weeks ago, Pirelli Construction was a dog-friendly workplace. Taking Rain along with him to the office and to job-site inspections kept the smart and curious puppy from being stuck at home by herself—bored and getting into trouble.

Which reminded him… Looking Rain in the eye, he said, "We owe a certain lady a new pair of shoes."

"What do you think?" Debbie asked Kayla as she stepped back to admire her handiwork.

"Frightfully delicious."

Debbie matched her assistant's grin. "Just what I was hoping you'd say."

The two of them were taking advantage of a midafternoon lull to decorate the bakery for Halloween. It was one of her favorite holidays, right up there with Christmas and Valentine's Day and—

Oh, who was she kidding? She loved any holiday associated with food, as the decorations throughout the bakery—black cats and witches and the occasional skeleton—would attest. But in keeping with the bakery, the silhouette of the arching cat taped to the front window was perched atop a black-and-white cupcake. And instead of stirring a caldron, the green-faced cartoon witch was whisking her potion in a mixing bowl.

The "spooky" decorations were a sharp contrast to the bakery's typically cheery atmosphere. Pink-and-white-striped valances hung over the front window and matching cushions decorated the tiny white bistro set, the only seating available within the small space. White bead board wainscoting lined the lower half of the walls, and the front of the checkout counter was topped by white marble. Frothy pink-frosted vanilla cupcakes floated across the white walls—murals Debbie had painted while her mother was recovering from her first round of chemotherapy.

Looking at them now, Debbie suffered a twinge of embarrassment. She felt like an adult who still had her kindergarten artwork displayed on the refrigerator. But her mother had loved the whimsical cupcakes so much, she couldn't bring herself to paint over them. It would have been too much like wiping the memory of her mother's happiness away.

"Why don't you drape some of the black streamers across the front counter and display case, and I'll hang the rest of these from the ceiling," Debbie said as she gathered up the orange, yellow and white candy-corn cutouts.

"What about these?" Kayla wrinkled her nose as she waved a hand at the black plastic spiders.

Debbie laughed at the look on the younger woman's face. "Sam's son, Timmy, inspired me there. He's got a thing for bugs. I'm going to add them to just a few of the cupcakes in the display case. They'll be great decorations to go along with the sugar cookies shaped like witches and black cats. And the severed ladyfingers—those have always been such a hit."

The rolled, oblong cookies fit their name, and for the spooky holiday, Debbie added a touch of pink to one end for a painted fingernail and then dipped the other side in red food coloring. "The adults usually refrain, but the bloodthirsty boys love them."

Faking a shudder, Kayla grabbed the roll of black crepe paper. "I am so glad I have a girl."

"Are you taking Annabel to the Fall Fest this year?"

Kayla flashed Debbie a smile over her shoulder as she knelt down to tape the twisted lengths of crepe paper to the front of the counter. With her slight build, light brown hair and pale blue eyes, Kayla Walker had a quiet, unassuming personality that hid the determined, hardworking woman inside. When Kayla had come in looking for a job, Debbie had hired her thinking she would be doing Kayla a favor. But after only a few months, Debbie knew she'd gotten the better end of the bargain—an honest, loyal employee determined to learn as much as she could.

"Are you kidding?" The younger woman laughed. "Devon wouldn't miss it. I keep telling him Annabel's too young for trick-or-treating, but he insists she'll have a great time. Which makes me think he's going to eat all the candy."

Maneuvering the ladder into place, Debbie climbed the rungs to hang the dangling candy-corn decorations. "Have you found a costume for her yet?"

"We did! It's the cutest sunflower outfit. Of course, it's really just a green jumpsuit with a hood designed to look like a sunflower, but it's so adorable! I had to take half a dozen pictures of her just when we were trying it on in the store."

"I can't wait to see. The kids and their costumes are my favorite part, and I love the way the town goes all out for the festival. There is something for everyone. Games, pumpkin carving, music, more food booths than you'd think could fit in such a small space. It's a chance for all the families to get together and have a good time."

Families... Even as she said the word, Debbie felt the slight ache in her chest. Oh, sure, she had great friends. Important, meaningful friendships, but family was something missing from her life.

We always wanted more children, her mother had told her once. Or maybe Bonnie had been talking to Debbie's father as she gazed with a lingering sadness at the picture of her late husband.

Debbie still had that photo on her coffee table, the last one taken of her dad, an image of a brown-haired man in a Nirvana T-shirt and faded jeans leaning against the hood of his truck and laughing into the camera. Looking so young…as if he had his whole life in front of him.

Debbie didn't know what affect her father's presence might have had, but she'd grown up under the weight of his absence. The feeling that life was short and could pass by all too quickly. So even though she might have felt a twinge or two when she thought of Kayla's adorable daughter, she pushed that longing aside.

Selfish as it may sound, she was going to focus on herself. She was going to have fun and enjoy a life free of commitment and responsibility while she still could. No one was going to tie her down until she was 100 percent ready. If taking over the bakery had taught her anything, it was that important lesson.

Bonnie's hope had been that her daughter would love running the bakery as much as she had, but as hard as she tried, Debbie didn't. And all the guilt in the world wasn't enough to smother the resentment that crept over her every now and then. The thought of settling down too soon and feeling that same resentment toward her husband or child… That fear alone would help her stand firm against any baby cravings.

Drew's dark eyes and sexy grin flashed through Debbie's mind, and a slight shiver raced through her body. A different kind of longing than the warm fuzzies she got when picturing little Annabel in her Halloween costume, for sure, but one she was just as determined to ignore.

Cooking breakfast for Drew the other morning had tugged hard at old dreams. She'd made him a massive omelet filled with diced ham, onions and peppers, enjoying every moment in his kitchen and well aware of his eyes following her every movement. She'd felt sexier there than she had ever felt with a man in the bedroom, and his over-the-top praise as he dug into the meal left her glowing with a far greater satisfaction, too.

Despite her acknowledgment that they were wrong for each other, her awareness of him on the ride back to The High Tide for her car had heightened her senses to an almost fevered pitch. She couldn't draw a breath without inhaling his scent. Couldn't stop herself from babbling inanely simply to hear the sound of his deep voice in response. Couldn't help resenting the seat belt that kept her on the opposite side of his SUV instead of pressed against him like she wanted to be.

But when she walked into work later that morning, she'd ruthlessly shoved her dreams of cooking for hungry guests—and other just-as-dangerous fantasies of making breakfast for Drew on a regular basis—aside.

Looking for something more than running the bakery— or for something more than friendship with Drew—would only led to heartbreak.

Pushing the thoughts aside, Debbie concentrated on the decorations. She and Kayla had just finished with the last of them when the timer from the kitchen buzzed. "Oh, those will be the cupcakes! I can't wait to try them. I bet they'll be amazing."

The younger woman led the way through the swinging door to the kitchen while Debbie followed at a slower pace. She had learned years ago how to tell when she'd found the perfect recipe. Long before she placed a cupcake or Danish or pie on display, she knew if the creation was just right or not. And it wasn't just a matter of taste that determined whether a new recipe was up to her standards.

It had to do with how the ingredients came together in the bowl—the texture, the color, the consistency. Even the scent of eggs, flour, vanilla and whatever other flavorings she might add. It was those "other flavors" that challenged her the most. She'd never been content, as her mother had once been, to simply offer the tried-and-true recipes she knew would sell.

Oh, sure, she always had those on hand, recipes she'd learned from her mother so long ago. Her chocolate-lovers' double-chocolate cake. Her traditional apple pie. Her always delicious vanilla cupcakes. And even though her mother had never been big on experimenting, it was while writing new recipes that Debbie best recalled standing at her mother's side enjoying the newness and wonder of learning to bake.

This afternoon, the experiment had been with more savory flavors as she tried to incorporate some of the fall-harvest vegetables into her cupcakes. The flavors of butternut squash and pumpkin combined with cinnamon and nutmeg, and she knew before she pulled the first tray from the oven just how they would taste.

"They're, um, different," Kayla said after she bit into one of the cakes before it had completely cooled. "But, you know...good," she clarified quickly.

"No, Kayla." Debbie sighed. "They're not."

"Sorry," Kayla ducked her head sheepishly. "It's not bad, but something's a little off. Or maybe I just like the traditional stuff—you know, vanilla and chocolate."

"Don't knock traditional stuff. It's what keeps us in business." And maybe she was only fooling herself in experimenting with bolder, more unusual recipes. Return customers came to Bonnie's Bakery with cravings for the familiar flavors they'd been savoring since her mother was alive. They weren't longing for different or exciting or unique—*she* was.

"Did you want me to stay and help with the prep work for tomorrow?" Kayla asked as Debbie slid the cupcakes onto one of the shelves on the stainless-steel cooling rack. She'd think on the recipe for a day or two and maybe come up with an answer for what was missing. A hint of cloves, maybe? More nutmeg and less cinnamon? Something sweet to balance the savory?

Pushing the thoughts aside for now, Debbie shook her head. "You've been covering for me in the mornings. I'll do the prep." Much of the dough—for cookies, pies and pastries—could be made the day before, cutting down on the predawn hours needed to keep the "baked fresh daily" promise. "Go spend time with that cute baby of yours."

Once Kayla left for the day, Debbie moved through the kitchen, performing tasks she could handle with her eyes closed. Creaming the softened butter and sugar, cracking the eggs, measuring out and adding the dry ingredients, transferring the dough to the butcher block counter and cutting into smaller sizes for easier handling.

The constant movement of her hands allowed her mind to wander to her plans for the bakery. If her extra promotion led to more orders for wedding and specialty cakes, would that help take away some of the monotony of her daily routine? Or would she only end up feeling overwhelmed by the more time-consuming, highly detailed work?

The piña colada cake for Nick and Darcy's wedding had been a specific request by the bride and groom. The tropical flavors were not traditional or for everyone, but Debbie thought the combination of coconut cream, pineapple and a hint of rum in the filling had been spot-on.

She'd spent hours on the painstaking work of piping

the basket-weave pattern, decorative flowers, bows and ribbons, wanting to give her friends the perfect cake, and she had received numerous compliments at the reception. Of course, most of the guests were friends and neighbors, people like Kayla who would be too polite or afraid of hurting her feelings to say anything negative. Other clients wouldn't be so kind.

She tried to stay focused on wedding cakes, but just the mere thought of weddings brought images of Drew to mind. His dark eyes sparkling as he met her gaze during her walk down the aisle. His tall, muscular body looking that much more masculine in the elegant tuxedo. The flash of his smile beneath the twinkling chandelier as he pulled her into his arms during their dance. His kiss on the balcony—

Debbie slammed the door on the memory. Hadn't she decided they were better off friends? That they were at different places in their lives and wanted different things? Wasn't that why she'd printed out the flyer advertising the next singles' event—karaoke night at The High Tide? She'd never dared to sing in public before, but she was ready to step out from her comfort zone. She wanted that hint of daring, of risk, of excitement in her life. She wanted—

A quick knock sounded at the back door, and her heart skipped a beat as Drew stepped inside. He'd clearly come from a job site—he looked rugged and outdoorsy in his work boots, faded jeans and a red-and-black-checkered flannel shirt over a gray T-shirt.

"Drew! What are you doing here?"

"I saw the kitchen lights were on from the front of the store and figured you were back here."

Sure enough, the late-afternoon sunlight had faded into darkness as she'd worked. But that really didn't explain why Drew had stopped by when the shop was already closed.

Not that she was afraid to be alone with him, but *knowing* that they were alone fired her awareness until she could feel each beat of her heart. He stepped closer and her breath caught on an inhale that drew in his scent—a mix of pine, fresh-cut wood, a hint of cool ocean air and warm, enticing man.

Reaching up, he brushed his thumb across her cheek. A slight stroke she felt down to her toes and every inch in between. "Drew…"

"You have some flour right here."

"I— Oh!" Flour, right. Of course. Why else would Drew be touching her? Ducking her head, Debbie scrubbed at her face, her skin suddenly hot with embarrassment and so much more. She'd hung a mirror behind the swinging door that lead to the bakery so she wouldn't end up greeting clients with flour on her face or chocolate around her mouth. But the mirror did little good when people surprised her by showing up at the back door.

Distracted, she didn't notice Drew reaching for the pumpkin cupcakes until it was too late. She started to protest, but he'd broken off a piece and popped it into his mouth before she could say a word. Served him right, she thought, hiding a smug smile, for sneaking treats from her kitchen.

He swallowed the bite, but not without pulling a face. "Sweetheart, you know I think you bake like a goddess, and your double-chocolate cake can bring a mortal man to his knees. But that—it needs some work."

"The recipe isn't ready yet," she admitted as she brushed by him. She pulled out the tray and focused on transferring the desserts into an airtight container so he wouldn't see how his words had affected her. She'd half expected him to try to spare her feelings by telling a white lie. She should have known better. His response had been simple and straightforward and honest. Funny, wasn't it, that his criticism made it easier for her to take his compliment to heart?

Drew thought she baked like a goddess.

And wouldn't she just love to believe she could bring him to his knees—only with something other than her skills in the kitchen? "I would have told you that had you actually asked to try them."

"Next time I'll remember. I'll even say please," he promised with a teasing grin just sexy enough to make a woman agree to anything—whether he said please or not.

A crumb clung to the corner of his mouth, and Debbie reached out before she could stop herself, brushing it aside with her thumb. He caught her hand with his, and for a moment, time hung suspended. Tension held her motionless even as she sucked in a quick breath. She caught a hint of coffee and chocolate—her cupcakes clearly weren't the only sweets he'd been sampling—and had the inane thought that she knew just how to fix the recipe.

A Drew-flavored cupcake... The product would fly off the shelves—if she didn't devour them all herself. Pulling her hand away, she took a step back and cleared her throat. "You do that, but for now, why don't you tell me why you're here. Assuming you didn't just stop by to steal cupcakes."

"I, um… No. I stopped by to bring you a present. Or maybe it's more of an IOU."

"Why would you owe me a present?" she asked as he ducked out the back door and came back in carrying a rectangular box.

"You'll see when you open it. Go on," he added as she hesitantly reached for the package.

The wrapping didn't give any clue as to what was inside,

but when she saw the box with the logo of her favorite shoe store hidden beneath the brown paper, she couldn't hide her smile. He hadn't! Debbie lifted the lid and brushed aside the crinkling white tissue paper. Oh, but he had! Reaching inside, she pulled out a pair of heels. They weren't the same as the ones Rain had turned into a chew toy the other night—with crisscrossing straps over the toe instead of the small bow—but it didn't matter.

The beige leather was butter soft to the touch, and it was all she could do not to kick off her practical white tie-ups. She already knew they would fit. Drew, being Drew, had of course bought the right size, and she couldn't wait to try them on.

"You didn't have to do this."

"They're not a perfect match for the other pair, but I hope they're a perfect fit."

"I love them. Thank you," she said, holding the shoes to her chest.

Of all the men in the world who she never thought could surprise her, Drew kept knocking her for a loop every time she turned around. Her resistance was melting, but Debbie couldn't let herself weaken. Drew Pirelli might be Clearville's perfect catch, but he was not the man for her.

"And Rain promises not to eat this pair."

"I'm sure she won't." Because, of course, the puppy wouldn't get the chance. After all, it wasn't like Debbie would be spending the night at Drew's again. And even if she did… She couldn't stop herself from remembering how she'd practically begged him to kiss her and how he'd teasingly turned her away.

Time for bed, princess.

She couldn't pretend the rejection hadn't hurt. He'd treated her like a kid when she longed to be treated like a woman. After playing the role of honorary big brother for so long, he couldn't see her any other way—their few exceptional kisses merely proving the rule.

"Thank you, again, for the shoes."

Drew frowned as Debbie nestled them back into the box. At first, she'd really seemed to like the gift, but now he wasn't so sure. He could have simply offered to pay for the shoes—that would have been the logical decision, but he'd wanted to do something more. Something that would make Debbie smile.

When he'd first walked in and seen her with her hair pulled back into a ponytail, a dusting of flour on her cheek, ten years had disappeared in a blink. Just seeing her looking like the adorable teenage girl he remembered had eased some of the pressure from his chest, the uncomfortable weight having settled there since the night of Darcy's bachelorette party. This was the Debbie he knew, the Debbie he was comfortable with, and he'd thought maybe she was right. Maybe the attraction he'd felt, the desire, had been nothing more than a lingering case of wedding fever and things between them could go back to normal now.

He'd even felt a little relieved at the thought, at the rational explanation that would keep his life moving forward on an even keel. And then she'd touched him....

Desire had slammed into his gut, knocking the breath from his lungs. All from her stroking her thumb across his mouth, and he knew he was only fooling himself if he thought life would ever be the same. He wanted her more than any woman ever before. Still coming to grips with the unexpected yet undeniable reaction, he'd tried to play it cool. Was still trying to play things cool when he glanced over her shoulder and saw a familiar-looking flyer stuck to the whiteboard beside the wall phone.

"What is this?" he demanded as he pulled the piece of paper out from beneath a teaspoon-shaped magnet.

Debbie gave a casual shrug as she placed the lid back on the shoebox. "It's an invitation to karaoke night with the singles' group. I thought it sounded fun."

"You've got to be kidding me! You still haven't changed you mind about—" Biting his tongue, Drew cut off the rest of his words. Debbie didn't know he'd overheard her wish the night of the bachelorette party and blurting it out now would not be the way to tell her. "After what happened last weekend, you're going out with that crowd again?"

"*Nothing* happened last weekend," she retorted, and was it his imagination or did she stress that first word a little too much?

Feeling the need to defend himself for turning away from the almost kiss, he said, "You had too much to drink. You weren't in any kind of shape to—"

"You don't have to worry about that," she interrupted. "I did get carried away, but I've learned my lesson. I won't drink, and I'll be perfectly sober when I decide who takes me home."

The flyer crinkled as his fingers tightened into a fist. No one was taking her home but him! "Debbie—"

Huffing out a sigh, she grabbed the now-wrinkled paper from his hand. Color brightened her cheeks and annoyance deepened her eyes to sapphire. "Give me a break, Drew! I'm just kidding. I want to go out and have some fun. I want to listen to horrible renditions of 'My Heart Will Go On.' I'm tired of my whole life revolving around work. I'm not like you. I'm not—"

"Not what?"

She sighed again. "It doesn't matter. This isn't about you. It's about me, and how I feel like my life is passing me by!"

"You're twenty-six years old! Your whole life is still in front of you."

"Is it? I turned twenty-six last month, and you know what? My dad never made it past twenty-five. I bet he thought he had his whole life in front of him, too, but then it was gone. Like that." She snapped her fingers in his face, but despite the defiant angle of her lifted chin, he could see the sorrow and lingering sadness in her gaze.

"Debbie, it's not the same thing."

"I know he had a dangerous job in a dangerous place, and I live and work in safe little Clearville, but that doesn't change knowing that life is short. And for the first time, I have the chance to go out and live it. Karaoke might sound stupid to you, but it's something I want to do. For me. Just because I can."

Listening to Debbie, that feeling was back—the urge to step out from his own comfort zone. To say the hell with playing it safe, to looking before he leaped, to weighing risk against reward. Maybe this was his opportunity, too, to go out and live life to the fullest. With Debbie by his side…because he couldn't imagine another woman who would inspire him to take such a chance.

His mind made up, he stepped closer, crowding her against the stainless-steel countertop until she had to tilt her head back to meet his gaze. "You aren't the only one who wants to have a good time, sweetheart, and you aren't the only one who signed up for the singles' group last weekend."

Her jaw dropped so comically he couldn't help reaching beneath her chin to guide it shut. He should have been better prepared, but her smooth skin against his work-roughened fingers packed as much punch the second time, and when she shivered in response… The faint tremor nearly knocked him to his knees, and he jerked his hand away before he embarrassed himself.

"What—what are you talking about?"

Playing it cool when he was feeling anything but, he answered, "Turns out I'm feeling hungry for the taste of adventure, too. I can't promise I'll sing any Celine Dion songs." Reaching out, he flicked the edge of the invitation she still held. "But I will see you there."

He backed out of the kitchen with a smile, enjoying the stunned look on Debbie's face. He figured he should escape while he still could before she came to her senses and smacked him upside the head. Or maybe before *he* came to his own and did it himself.

Karaoke? He *hated* karaoke. But he couldn't remember a night he was looking forward to more.

Maybe it didn't make any sense, but he still couldn't wipe the smile from his face. Debbie wanted a man who could take her by surprise? Well, he was pretty sure he'd succeeded. He had her off balance, but he was willing to bet he'd captured her curiosity, too. The longer he could stoke that flicker of interest and anticipation, the better.

His conscience dug at him a little, a reminder of the unfair advantage he had—having overheard Debbie's at the bachelorette party—but he pushed the concern aside. He would tell her the truth…just not yet.

Chapter Six

"So do you think he'll be here tonight?"

The words had been echoing on such a constant loop since Drew had left the bakery the night before that it took a moment for Debbie to realize they weren't just in her head. Glancing over to her right, she met the curious gaze of a brunette who looked to be in her early thirties. Recognizing her, Debbie said, "It's Marcy, right? You were here for the meet and greet."

The other woman nodded. "I figured I'd give it another shot even though last weekend was a bit of a bust. Well, for everyone but you. So is he coming tonight?"

"I don't—"

"Oh, come on! Don't pretend you can't remember the tall, dark and gorgeous guy who couldn't take his eyes of you?"

Tall, dark and handsome… The night of Darcy's bachelorette party, that was exactly the way she'd described her fantasy guy—the one who was supposed to take her by surprise and fill her life with romance and excitement. Funny, wasn't it, that those same words so perfectly described Drew?

"He, um, said he would be," she responded.

"Thought so by the way you're looking over at the door every thirty seconds."

She wasn't, was she? Debbie mentally groaned. Okay, so physically Drew met the criteria of her perfect man, but as for the rest— "I really don't think he's my type," she told Marcy.

The other woman gave a snort of laughter. "In that case, I'd be afraid to see who *is* your type."

Debbie fought back a sigh. The whole point of joining the singles' group was so she could meet someone new and exciting…but wasn't there something different about Drew lately?

The Drew she knew—the Drew she *thought* she knew— wouldn't have kissed her on the balcony the night of Nick and Darcy's wedding. He would never have gotten so carried away by the moment that he forgot where they were or that half the town was gathered on the other side of the French doors. Never would have picked her up off her feet, kissed her and carried her off to his SUV.

And the Drew she knew wouldn't be walking into The High Tide on karaoke night, looking gorgeous enough in a pair of dark jeans and slate-gray sweater to stop her heart and steal her breath…

No, this just wasn't the Drew she knew at all.

His dark eyes scanned the corner of the restaurant reserved for the singles' group, and she could tell the moment he spotted her. He stopped looking, stopped everything, freezing as their gazes met and held, and she could almost believe he was struck by the same jolt of attraction that she felt for him. He smiled then, the tilt of his lips a little wry as if he too was surprised he'd shown up.

"Oh, no," Marcy murmured at Debbie's side, "you two aren't into each other at all."

Debbie didn't try to explain to the other woman something she didn't understand herself. But as she watched Drew stride toward her, she couldn't help wondering if she was so wrong about him…could that mean he was so right for her?

"Well, someone's gotta get this party started," Marcy said with a nod toward the DJ manning the karaoke machine. "You're singing, too, aren't you?"

For a split second, Debbie broke her focus from Drew and glanced over at the blue television screen waiting for the first brave soul to step up to the microphone. "I haven't decided on a song yet." A huge three-ring binder sat on the table, offering just about every well-known and not-so-well-known single ever recorded.

"Ah, don't overthink things. Just go for it," the other woman advised with a wink as she pushed away from the table just as Drew approached, and Debbie had to wonder if the brunette was still talking about finding the right song.

"Don't tell me I already missed your solo." Sinking into the chair beside her, he leaned back, his long legs stretched out in front of him. He looked totally relaxed and comfortable, as if the two of them were buddies hanging out at the bar, while she felt ready to jump out of her skin.

Was she only imagining that Drew felt something more? Setting herself up to fall for a guy only to have him tell her they were better off friends? It wouldn't be the first time.

She swallowed hard, but the ache in her throat and the pressure in her chest didn't go away. Bad enough Robert had dumped her following their one night together. How much worse would it be if Drew did the same thing?

Maybe she should quit while she was ahead. So she and Drew had shared a few kisses. It didn't have to mean anything. She could keep those good memories and not have to worry about them tarnishing later.

Drew moved closer as the music kicked up and Marcy started to sing—a decent rendition of Adele belting out that they could have had it all. His dark eyes snared hers as he said, "Don't tell me you've changed your mind."

Had she? Caught by her own indecision, Debbie wished she had some kind of sign from Drew that she wasn't alone in this longing.

"I'd hate to think I missed you promising that your heart will go on." He raised an eyebrow in challenge. "Or were you waiting for me?"

Debbie managed a laugh. "Waiting for you? I didn't think you'd even show."

"Yeah," he murmured, leaning in until she could feel the warm caress of his breath against her ear. "You did."

"What makes you so sure?" She made the mistake of turning to face him as she issued her challenge, and her breath caught as she realized his face was mere inches away, his mouth within easy kissing distance.

"You're wearing my shoes."

Her face heated, and she couldn't pretend she hadn't been thinking of him as she'd dressed for the evening. Couldn't pretend she hadn't been thinking of him almost nonstop since Nick and Darcy's wedding. Striving for some semblance of cool—without giving away her sanity-saving need to retreat—Debbie leaned back in her chair. "Seeing as you gave them to me to replace the ones I bought, I think that makes them mine now."

"Whatever you say, sweetheart. I'm still willing to bet you were counting on me showing tonight."

"Yeah, well, I'm starting to think I'm not the betting type."

"Oh, we both know that's not true. You've always been the type to take risks."

"Me?" She laughed again, this time the sound filled with unbelief. "Since when?"

"For as long as I've known you. You were always the one to go against the pack, to speak your own mind, to stand up for the kids in school who wouldn't defend themselves. I think you were the only one of Sophia's friends to stick by her when all that business with vandalism at Hope's shop went down."

Five years ago, his sister had been convinced by a friend of hers to sneak into The Hope Chest—the local antiques store owned by Hope Daniels. Sophia hadn't known her supposed friends had planned to rob and ransack the place once they were inside. Nor had she known that Hope was staying in the small apartment above the shop. The older woman had been injured when she'd gone down to investigate the break-in. The rest the teens had scattered, but Sophia had stayed behind until the paramedics arrived to help Hope, even though it meant getting caught red-handed and taking the blame.

"I knew Sophia wasn't responsible for that. She never would have done anything to hurt Hope."

"A lot of people probably believed that, but none of them were as vocal about their faith in her as you were. Sophia always appreciated that. So did the rest of us."

The rest of us... Drew meant the rest of his family. In many ways, the Pirellis had been like family to Debbie since her mother had become ill and especially after her death. They looked out for her, inviting her to family get-togethers and holiday parties as if she was one of their own. As an only child, she'd often envied her friends' large and loving family. A family just like the one Drew no doubt wanted for himself—sooner rather than later.

"I never saw any of that as taking a risk, but even if it is, I'm not—"

"Willing to take a chance on me? On us?"

Us... Debbie swallowed. She'd asked for a sign, and that was a pretty big one, lit up in glowing green letters that had her hormones wanting to charge full speed ahead. But still she hesitated. "I don't think— We don't want the same things, Drew."

"And yet we're both here tonight."

"I'm not talking about tonight. I'm talking about the future. I'm not interested in settling down right now. I don't want a relationship. I just want to go out and have fun and be free to live *my* life."

Tilting his head, he studied her until she fought to shift under the intense scrutiny. "Weren't you the one to remind me that you can't count on the future? That you never know what might happen today?"

Debbie didn't know why she'd brought up her father the other day. She rarely talked about him. He was little more than a memory, and she'd never been certain if the memories were her own or just stories told so often by her mother that they'd become almost real.

For other people, turning twenty-six might not have been such a milestone, but it had hit her hard. Hard enough to make her question what she was doing with her life. Or, more specifically, what she *wasn't* doing with it.

As long as she could remember, she'd lived with the awareness that life was short. Yet somehow she'd still let some of the best years—her teens and early twenties— pass by while she struggled just to get through one day and onto the next.

She half expected to see pity in Drew's dark gaze, but

instead saw only understanding, as if he knew exactly what she was thinking and why she'd set out on this mission to seize the day. And rather than trying to talk her out of it, he was waiting...for her.

But that wasn't possible. Was it?

"You want me to take a chance on us, but there is no 'us,' Drew," she pointed out, almost desperately. "There's me and the woman I really am, and then there's you and the kid you still think I am."

"I admit it took a while for me to see how much you've changed. You've been my kid sister's best friend for as long as I've known you, and it was easier for me to keep you in that role. Safer."

Right! Debbie barely swallowed a sarcastic laugh. Like she posed any danger to a man like Drew. No matter what he said, she was the girl next door, not the femme fatale. All the karaoke in the world wouldn't change that.

"You're wrong, though, if you think I still see you as a kid or that my feelings for you are platonic. And you're wrong if you don't think I want to kiss you right now more than I've ever wanted anything."

Her pulse pounded so wildly in her throat, she couldn't swallow, couldn't breathe. *Simple, straightforward, honest.* The words she'd used to describe Drew the other day still rang true. If he said he wanted her...

"It's your turn," he said softly.

Her turn to do what exactly? To spill her feelings like he'd just done? Or maybe... Debbie dropped her gaze to his lips as she wondered if his words were an invitation to do what she'd wanted to do since he'd sat down beside her.... Her heart was still pounding, but over the raging beat, she heard someone call her name. Blinking, she jerked out of the fantasy of kissing Drew and realized half the people around her were staring at her. "My—what?"

"Come on, Debbie!" Marcy called out. She still held the microphone but was pointing it in Debbie's direction. "It's your turn." The brunette's grin was broad, and Debbie could see her name printed in bold letters across the screen.

A wave of sheer panic washed over her. Oh, no. She couldn't do this. All those people staring at her as she opened her mouth to sing... What if she screwed up? What if her voice went flat and the words came out all wrong? Or worse, what if she froze and couldn't make a sound? Heat crawled up her face, and she didn't think she could breathe, forget trying to sing. Suddenly light-headed, she struggled to pull in a gasp of air. "I don't think—"

"Don't think," urged Drew. "Just go up there."

The irony of Drew's advice was enough to shake off some of the terror. "Funny, coming from you. When do you ever act first and think later?"

His grin was wry as he pulled her off the stool and to her feet. "You'd be surprised. Now go do this."

A tiny stage had been set up in the corner of the room, complete with a spotlight ready to showcase her utter humiliation. "Drew—"

His large, warm hand gripped the back of her neck and kissed just long enough to leave her breathless and just short enough to leave her longing for more. "I promise you, I will be thinking about that later. Now go knock 'em dead."

"That was so much fun!" Debbie grinned as she stepped out into the night air, her arms thrown out wide as she spun to face him. "I can't believe you didn't get up and sing!"

"Maybe next time."

Whether she realized it or not, tonight hadn't been about him. This had been her night, and man, had she shone. Drew still couldn't understand why she'd hesitated to go up on stage. How had he not known Debbie had such an amazing voice, and watching her on stage *watching* him as she performed—

He'd never seen a sexier sight.

It didn't matter that the songs had been pop tunes— "Girls Just Wanna Have Fun," her opening number and a theme she clearly embraced. What counted was seeing the light in her eyes and the confidence she gained as she broke away from the past and reclaimed a piece of herself that she'd lost along the way.

"Marcy was really good, too, wasn't she?" Debbie asked as she waved at the brunette from across the now-deserted parking lot. The two women had pretty much closed down the place, and only a few cars remained. "Kurt asked her out," she said of the sandy-haired man walking with the other woman. "I think they make a cute couple."

"Mmm-hmm." Drew wasn't really interested in which of the singles had paired up that night. He was just glad the other guys had given Debbie a wide berth after he'd sat down beside her. After he'd kissed her, they'd backed off entirely.

If he'd known that was all it would take— Hell, he should have kissed Debbie a long time ago, and not just as a way to warn off other single guys.

Her eyes had deepened to sparkling sapphire and her hair gleamed almost silver in the misty moonlight. A pair of white jeans hugged her hips, and she was wearing a red sweater that reminded him of the candy apples from his youth. Debbie might not care for the description, but just looking at her had his mouth watering for something sweet. Her gaze softened as she gazed over at Marcy and her new potential boyfriend, Kurt.

Drew's gut tightened at the wistful smile tilting her lips. Was she wishing she'd met someone tonight? That some new, not-Clearville guy was walking her to her car, getting her number and making plans to see her again?

She noticed him watching her and glanced away, her expression somewhat guilty. Was she embarrassed that he'd caught her daydreaming about the kind of guy she had yet to find?

Debbie had complained that the guys in town only saw her as a little sister. Could it be that she only saw him in that same platonic light? Every masculine muscle in his body tensed at the idea. Yes, she'd returned his kiss tonight and at the wedding, but both times he'd caught her off guard, ambushing her even. He knew he was the exact opposite of everything she said she wanted—but could he change her mind?

"Do you ever wonder," she began, only to send her blond hair tumbling back over her shoulders as she shook her head. "Never mind."

"Wonder what?" he pressed.

"Do you ever wonder what might have happened if we'd met on a night like tonight? If we hadn't practically grown up together but instead were brought together by singles' night like Marcy and Kurt. Two strangers whose eyes meet across a crowded bar." Debbie laughed at the cliché, but the question lingered in her expression.

Strangers meeting in a bar… That was the fantasy she'd described during Darcy's bachelorette party. On that night, he wasn't supposed to have heard her wish, but tonight—Drew's heartbeat quickened. Did he dare see her words as encouragement, that she was putting *him* in the role? Taking a chance, he said, "I don't have to wonder."

"You don't?"

"I know what would have happened."

"You do?" Debbie made a face as if acknowledging the way she'd taken to echoing everything he was saying.

"First I would tell you how amazing you were on stage tonight and what a great voice you have."

Her lips twitched a smile she gave him a sideways glance. "You already did that."

"Good. That means I'm right on track."

"And what comes next?"

"Well, I'd offer to walk you to your car, of course," he said just as they reached her lime-green VW Bug.

"Very chivalrous of you."

He made a soft sound of agreement. "See, if you knew me better and if I wasn't a total stranger, you'd realize that I am very much a gentleman."

Her smile glowed even brighter as he played along with the game of pretend she'd established. "And once we reached my car…" She placed a hand on the shiny hood as she turned to face him. "What would you do then? Would you ask for my phone number? Would you kiss me good-night?"

Drew stepped close and then closer until he could feel the heat from Debbie's body calling out to his. "Oh, yeah," he answered, his voice dropping an octave as his gaze fell to her lips, parted and waiting beneath his. "I would definitely want to see you again. And only an idiot wouldn't kiss you if he had the chance."

Her eyes widened at his reference to the weekend before when he hadn't kissed her and had turned away instead. But that was then and this was now. Tonight Debbie hadn't had anything stronger to drink than iced tea. And after tonight, he better understood what was motivating her to go down this path.

This wasn't some whim that had struck Debbie during the bachelorette party, even if that was when she'd first given voice to her longing for something more. This was important to her, and for reasons Drew couldn't completely understand, it was important to him to help her fulfill that wish. He didn't bother trying to fool himself into believing he was simply trying to look out for her, and though that protective instinct was still on guard inside him, somehow the feeling had changed...grown.

Keeping Debbie safe wasn't as important as making her happy.

Drew's conscience gave a snort of laughter. All the logic and reasoning he came up with might help justify his actions and keep him from feeling too guilty about coming on to a woman he'd always treated like family, but logic and reason carried little weight against one simple fact.

He wanted to kiss her more than he wanted to draw his next breath.

But despite her bold and flirty words, the moonlight touched on the hesitation in her expression, and Drew could have kicked himself for the way he'd rejected her before. He'd had his reasons, good ones he'd thought, but he'd hurt her, and that was the last thing he ever wanted to do.

Settling his hands on her shoulders, he bent his head and put his whole heart in making this kiss everything their first should have been. A slow study as he experienced the warmth and sweetness of her mouth. A learning curve as he discovered the shape of her lips with his own and sought to determine what she liked—but then slow and sweet seemed to slip from his fingers along with his control, and he found himself wrapping his arms around her and holding her tight.

They were both breathless by the time he stepped back. He might have felt a sense of masculine satisfaction at the unfocused look in her eyes if he wasn't having so much trouble seeing straight himself. Blinking, she lifted a hand to touch her lips. "That, um, that was some first kiss."

He tried to answer, barely managing a grunt in response.

Still partially hidden by her fingers, Debbie's mouth curved into a smile. A confident smile, one that erased any sign of the vulnerability he'd sensed in her earlier. The sight was almost enough to make Drew overlook that she'd recovered faster than he had from that mind-blowing kiss. Who exactly, he wondered, was seducing whom?

"You know, if we had met tonight for the first time, I think I just might give you my number."

"Might?" he bit out in a disbelieving laugh. "You *might* give it to me?"

"Yep," she answered with a saucy wink as she opened her car door and slid behind the wheel.

Reaching out, Drew caught the edge of the door and leaned down until they were face-to-face. "And what if I gave you mine?"

Her husky laughter hit like a sucker punch to his gut. "Oh, I think we both know I've already got that."

Chapter Seven

The knock at the bakery's back door was the answer to her prayer, and Debbie let the soaking-wet mop fall into a pile of soggy towels as she rushed across the kitchen. "Thank goodness you're here!"

Drew greeted her with a cocky grin, one hand braced against the jamb, the other carrying a toolbox. "You know, when you said you had my number, I didn't really think you'd be using it so soon."

Her face heating, she tried to act cool and knew she was failing miserably as he stepped inside the disaster that was now her kitchen. "Trust me, neither did I."

At least not like this. She'd had a nightmare of an afternoon and Drew—Drew looked like every red-blooded woman's fantasy man come true. He could have stepped right out from a "Men at Work" calendar. A leather tool belt hung low on his lean, denim-clad hips and a faded green henley T-shirt embraced his broad shoulders and flat abs. But Drew was the real deal, and the scarred belt and work-worn boots were more than simple props.

So unfair, when she was almost as big of a mess as her bakery kitchen.

"I just went to adjust the sprayer on the faucet," she said, waving at the double-bowl industrial sink, "and the whole thing came off in my hand and water started shooting out all over the place! I tried the shutoff valve but it was too tight to move, and by the time I'd grabbed a wrench, water was everywhere, and it was all I could do to move the flour and sugar out of the way to keep it from getting ruined."

The fifty-pound bags were hard enough to lift under the best of conditions. Hauling them out from the pantry during a sudden flood had left Debbie a tired, sweaty, *soggy* mess. Her first thought that didn't involve a dozen or so swear words had been to call Drew.

Only now that he was here, she wished she'd called someone—anyone—else. She wanted him to see her as the woman she'd been the other night. Confident, bold, sensual. Instead she felt like reality had once again come crashing down on her dreams, reminding her that this— the bakery, life in Clearville and her role as Drew's kid sister's friend—was all there'd ever be.

"You didn't have to come over. I thought you'd just recommend someone," she said finally. "I'm sure you have bigger projects to bother checking on my faulty plumbing."

"No job is too small, and I still like getting my hands dirty."

Okay, that should not have sounded so sexy, but feeling like she did, she couldn't come up with a witty comeback. His teasing grin faded at her silence, and Drew set the toolbox down before stepping closer. He cupped her face in his hands, and it was all Debbie could do not to duck away from his searching gaze.

She didn't want him seeing her looking like this. Didn't want to watch the realization *she'd* just had steal across his features. And his expression did change—but not into one of pity or regret. A warmth and caring filled his dark eyes, so strong she could feel it in the brush of his thumbs against her cheeks, in the massaging fingers that tunneled into her hair.

"And I didn't want to send someone else. I wanted to be here. To be the one to play the white knight and ride in to save the day."

Debbie managed a smile as he turned the words she used the night of the meet and greet against her. "Sorry, Drew, but I'm not exactly feeling like a fairy-tale princess right now."

"And I can't think of a better moment to come to your rescue."

She knew she was a total mess, and yet the look in his eyes— He'd looked at her the same way the night before— when she'd spent an hour on her hair and makeup. Desire and awareness swirled through his eyes....

This time she did duck away, too afraid Drew would see the tears in her eyes at his murmured words. But that only made it easier for him to pull her into his arms and tuck her head beneath his chin. She felt the brush of his lips against her hair, but the sweetness of the kiss only made her feel cherished. She didn't know how long he held her. All she knew was that she could have stayed in his arms forever.

"So are you going to let me help you clean up this place? Please?"

"Well, since you did say please," she said with a watery laugh. She pulled out of his embrace, blinking back tears, and glanced around at the mess in the kitchen that suddenly didn't seem so bad. With Drew working by her side, they had the wet towels spinning in the washer and the last of the water mopped up from the floor within minutes.

"How badly do you need water right now? Are you right in the middle of anything?"

"No, actually. I was just cleaning up when the faucet broke." She waved a hand at the covered bowls of batter waiting to be poured into muffin tins and baked. "Those are all ready to go."

"Uh-oh." Drew warily eyed the orange batter. "Those aren't the same cupcakes from the other day, are they?"

"No. I told you those weren't ready yet."

Before the broken faucet and minor flood, she'd been elbow deep in fixing the recipe she'd tried out the other day. With the disaster averted and her breakdown under control, anticipation surged through her as she thought of the cupcakes waiting to be baked. Waiting to be tasted. Her pulse picked up its pace as she anticipated Drew's reaction.

Building on the base foundation of the recipe, she'd taken it in a half a dozen different directions. She couldn't wait for him to sample them all, couldn't wait to see his expression as she teased his taste buds with minicupcakes that were little more than a bite and guaranteed to leave him wanting more....

"Okay, then. I'll replace the faucet while you throw those cupcakes in the oven, and when they're done..."

"I'll let you try them," she promised even as she wondered at the excitement brewing inside her. Was this the spark, then, that had been missing from the bakery these past few years? Simply having someone to share it with?

Debbie wished the answer could be so simple. But she and Kayla had sampled plenty of recipes, new ones and old favorites as she taught her young apprentice, and it hadn't been enough to light this kind of fire in her oven. The idea that only Drew could stoke the flames of passion in her was too troubling to contemplate, so she shoved the thought aside.

"But I want you to tell me the truth. These are still new recipes, and if you don't like them, I want you to say so. I would never expect you to love everything I make. And I'd much rather you tell me the truth than convince me those cupcakes were wonderful when they're not."

"Really?"

"Really. If you're honest about what you don't like, then I know I can trust you when you say you do like something. It might sound funny, but that means a lot to me, Drew."

She'd been on her own for so long she'd learned to trust her own judgment, but would it really be so bad to have someone else to count on? Not all the time, but just every now and then?

Drew broke her gaze, and Debbie wondered if she'd embarrassed him with her praise. "Debbie, I—" Cutting himself off, he shook his head. "I'm gonna go grab a faucet. I'll have the old one replaced in no time."

"Okay, you go do your job while I do mine."

"I should warn you, I tend to work up an appetite doing hard, manly labor like this."

Debbie grinned. "I'm counting on it."

I know I can trust you… That means a lot to me, Drew.

After making a run to the hardware store, Drew returned to the bakery and tried staying focused on the job. But the hardest part was maneuvering his large frame into the cramped space beneath the sink. The work itself wasn't nearly challenging enough to keep his mind off Debbie— or to keep the guilt from burning away inside him.

The trust shining in her eyes as she gazed up at him hit hard. Not that he was lying to her, exactly. He was just— Drew swore as the wrench slipped off the bolt and his knuckles scraped against the plaster wall. Who was he trying to kid? He was lying to her. By omission, but lying all the same.

He should have come clean by now about overhearing her the night of the bachelorette party. He *would* tell her, before they took things any further, or the guilt would eat him alive. But he had to find the right moment when she'd be open to listening to his explanation and not jump to the conclusion that he'd manipulated the situation. That he'd used her own words against her or—even worse— used her.

A mouthwatering, fresh-from-the-oven smell—a hint of spice and sweetness that reminded him of Debbie's own scent—filled the kitchen. She'd finished baking the cupcakes while he was at the store and had stuck them in the freezer to cool quickly while she made the frosting.

"These are just about ready," she said as she drizzled something across the top of the cupcakes. "Are you at a stopping point?"

"Nope. I'm all finished." He turned on the new faucet with a flick of the handle.

"Oh, perfect timing!"

She flashed a smile at him, and Drew had the thought that his timing wasn't the only thing that was perfect—*she* was. He knew she hated the girl-next-door image, but there was a sweetness and friendliness about her that couldn't be denied. And for too long, that was all he had seen. But beyond the blond hair, blue eyes and bubbly laughter, Debbie was tough. Resilient, a fighter who'd battled through life's hardships and hidden so much of what she was feeling behind a smile. Maybe too much. She was right when she said she could take care of herself, but he wanted to be the one to take care of *her*.

"Come on. I can't wait for you to taste this."

His gaze automatically dropped to her lips, and he swallowed. Hard. "Yeah, um, give me a second to clean up." He washed his hands quickly, wincing slightly at the sting of water and soap against his scraped knuckles. Less than he deserved, his conscience berated him, for not *truly* coming clean.

But one look in her sparking blue eyes and his plan to tell the truth stalled. The words got caught behind the lump in his throat as he realized how much *he* wanted to be the one to put that spark in her eyes. The one to keep her on her toes when he wasn't sweeping her off her feet—and no short-term fling was going to do.

"Drew? Are you okay?" Debbie asked.

A frown knit her eyebrows together, and he realized he'd been standing motionless even as the earth shifted beneath his feet. "I, um, yeah. I was just—making sure the faucet's running right." Reaching out, he shut off the tap. "You should probably have all the plumbing checked out." Logic may have deserted him, but at least he still had the job to fall back on. "The wiring, too. You know how old these buildings are."

"As long as the faucet's no longer acting like a fountain, everything's good. Rattling pipes and flickering lights are all part of the turn-of-the-century charm. Now come on! I can't wait for you to try this new recipe."

Still stunned by his realization, when Debbie reached out and grabbed his hand she could have led him straight into traffic and he wouldn't have put up a fight. Thankfully, she simply led him to the counter where she had arranged several different plates. Each one showed off a minicupcake with carefully piped frosting swirled over the top. He'd seen her do something similar before—when she'd offered Nick and Darcy a taste test for their wedding cake.

The ground shifted beneath his feet again even though the plates held cupcakes and not slices of wedding cake. Bracing a hand against the stainless-steel counter, he sucked in a deep breath and prayed the world would quickly right itself once more. Fortunately, Debbie seemed completely unaware of the earthshaking, life-altering moments as she reached for the first plate.

"Now, the batters for all of these are mostly the same, but each one has some slight differences. I already know which one is my favorite, but I want to see what you think. And remember, be completely honest."

At first, Drew wasn't sure he'd be able to swallow a single bite, but that wasn't giving Debbie nearly enough credit. With the first taste, he knew the tiny dessert would never be enough. Unlike the cupcake he'd tasted the other day, which had been heavy and dense, this one was light and moist with flavors that perfectly captured the rich flavors of an autumn day. The pumpkin-spice cupcake was filled with bits of walnut and dried fruit and topped with butterscotch icing so good that he wanted to lick the last crumb from the plate.

"That's it. That has to be your favorite."

Debbie shook a teasing finger at him. "No fair choosing until you've tasted them all."

"I don't know what you did with the recipe, but as far as I'm concerned, it's perfect now."

"Hard to tell they're somewhat healthy, too, isn't it?"

"Seriously?"

"Yep. I've been experimenting with an entire line of health-conscious desserts for my online menu. Did you know in some of the bigger cities, there are bakeries that sell cakes that are one-hundred-percent gluten-free? They use rice flour for people with allergies that make eating the typical desserts impossible. Some places have gone organic, too, or even vegan, using applesauce in cakes rather than eggs."

"So why are you only offering those desserts online?"

"Oh, come on, Drew. You know what it's like around here. No one wants to see Bonnie's Bakery change."

Bonnie's Bakery. It was odd after years of knowing one another to realize there were things about Debbie he didn't know. Things he'd never thought to ask—like why she'd kept the name of the bakery. "Is it Clearville that doesn't want the bakery to change," he asked gently, "or is it you?"

"What do you mean?" Wariness and a flash of something buried deeper rippled beneath the surface of her expression.

In anyone else, Drew would have labeled the expression fear, but he'd never known Debbie to be afraid of anything. Wasn't protecting her from charging off into adventure and excitement what started him down this road?

"The front of the bakery, the uniform…" Reaching out, he tugged on the collar, and then couldn't resist brushing his thumb against her jaw. Her cheeks heated until the color almost matched the pink of the shirt. Her soft-as-silk skin made him forget why he'd reached out in the first place. Made him forget everything but the urge to cup her face in his hands and bring her mouth to his. To have a taste test of his own and determine once and for all what was most irresistible—the flavor of her parted lips, the delicate curve behind her jaw, the hidden valley between her breasts…

"The uniform?"

Her echoed words dragged him back from his heated thoughts, and a decade-old memory surfaced. How Debbie had complained to Sophia not long after she'd first started working behind the counter.

I look like a strawberry ice cream cone, she'd said. *Pink on top and tan on the bottom.*

Ten years on, and Drew doubted her opinion of the shirt and pants had improved, and yet she still wore them every day at work. "The uniform. Even the name," he finished. "You haven't changed any of it."

"This was my mother's dream, and keeping the name is my way of keeping that dream alive. It was her bakery long before I took over, and she loved it."

And Debbie didn't.

The thought startled Drew, but he realized it was true. Just because she baked like a dream and greeted every customer who walked into her shop with a smile, he'd assumed running the bakery was all she'd ever wanted to do. He'd never asked, never even considered, that she might have wanted something different—something more....

Could the excitement and adventure she was seeking in her personal life be due in part to feeling so stifled professionally? If Debbie felt free to branch out at the bakery, might she then be more willing to settle down into a relationship? Say, a relationship with him?

To Drew, it all made sense, though he couldn't help wondering if he wasn't twisting logic so Debbie's vision of the future would dovetail into his own. One thing he knew was that trying to force those pieces to fit wouldn't work. He'd have to be patient, something that had never been a problem for him in the past. So why did he already feel so restless?

Maybe because wanting Debbie, wanting that future, was so much bigger, so much more important than anything he'd wanted before....

For now, he'd settle for seeing that spark back in her eyes, one that had dimmed as they talked about her mother, so he was glad when she responded by teasing, "And when I thought about changing the name, I got stuck on the whole alliteration thing and I just couldn't get around Debbie's Donuts."

"Debbie's Donuts...Mattson's Muffins," he supplied.

"So you see my dilemma."

"I do," he agreed. But solving it would have to wait for another day. Once he'd considered how he could encourage Debbie to reach for her own dreams while still holding true to her mother's. "I hope you understand my dilemma, too."

"What's that?"

"How I'm supposed to pick just one favorite," he said as he reached for another plate.

The spark was back as Drew quickly devoured three more minicupcakes—one with chunks of toffee inside and a matching frosting, another with macadamia nuts and a white-chocolate icing and the last with a hint of orange. Though they all were delicious, none could beat the first one, but Debbie was wearing a secret smile as she reached for the final plate.

"I probably shouldn't say anything since I don't want to influence your opinion but...this is my favorite." She lifted the minicupcake, stepping close enough for him to feel her body heat and to catch a hint of her scent—as delicious and tempting as anything she'd ever made in this kitchen. Did she know, he wondered, that she was doing so much more than influencing his *opinion?* From that seductive, secret smile, he'd bet she did.

And what was that old saying? If you can't take the heat...

Well, they were already in the kitchen.

Drew raised a hand, but instead of taking the cake from Debbie, he wrapped his fingers around hers and guided her hand to his mouth. The combination of flavors—a hint of pumpkin and spice mixed with chunks of dark chocolate and a shot of coffee—was to die for. But it was the mix of emotions on her face—awareness, anticipation, desire—that had him coming back for more. He savored the tiny dessert, making it last bite after bite, until there was nothing left to do but lick the last traces of frosting from her fingers....

The tug and pull of his mouth against her skin send a rush of sweet, rich heat pouring through Debbie's veins. The sensation pooled in her belly and sapped strength, turning her bones to molten chocolate. Her legs trembled and her head tipped back. All that from his mouth against her fingers. Just the thought of those skilled lips teasing and tormenting more intimate flesh...

A delicious shiver racked her whole body. Drew's dark gaze held her captive—watching and knowing just what he was doing to her—and yet she couldn't look away. "Drew."

His name was little more than a gasp for breath and his answer little more than a wicked grin. "Looks like you were right."

"I was?" She swallowed hard, trying to gather her scrambled wits. "Oh, good. I always like being right. What is it I'm right about again?"

His grin grew even bigger and even more wicked. "This is my favorite."

Debbie didn't know if he was talking about tasting the cupcakes or tasting *her,* but then he was kissing her and she couldn't think at all. He framed her face in his hands as he deepened the kiss, his fingers splayed wide, as if he felt the same desperation to touch, to taste, to experience all he could in a stolen moment of time.

She slid her hands up his back, the material of his shirt denying the skin-against-skin friction she craved. She fisted her hands, but warm cotton was no substitute for hot skin. He pulled her tight, and she no longer cared that her bones were melting because it made it so much easier for him to meld her body to his. Her curves met the hardened planes and angles of his masculine form—softening, conforming, blending with a sense of perfection she'd never experienced before.

The panicked feeling came out of nowhere, a cold splash of reality. She didn't want perfect or permanent or lasting. She wanted— Drew's mouth trailed across her cheek, his breathing as ragged and gasping as her when she moaned his name.

She wanted Drew.

No. Well, yes, she wanted him. But she couldn't— wouldn't—fall for him. Not because it would be hard, but because it would be all too easy.

"This is crazy," she breathed, knowing it wouldn't take much more for her whole body to break from the sheer pleasure. She was barely aware of speaking the words. She certainly hadn't meant them as a criticism, but Drew stilled, caught on the razor's edge that gripped them both.

Oh, please, let this be happening to both of them.

His breath was hot, rasping, against her shoulder. The tension held his body tight to hers, but Debbie's awareness gradually expanded from the circle of Drew's arms to their surroundings—the batches of cupcakes she still needed to frost, the icing likely hardening in the bowls, the kitchen Bonnie had treated like sacred ground. Her mother would be scandalized.

Drew slowly straightened away from her, humor banking some of the heat in his gaze. "I'm starting to think crazy is a good thing."

The so un-Drewlike statement startled a laugh from her. "Since when?" she asked as the moment of levity eased the pressure on her chest and cooled some of the raging desire.

At least until he answered, "Since I haven't been able to

get you out of my head. Since I can't stop thinking about the next time I'll have you in my arms again."

A hint of a question lingered in his words. Asking for a next time? Or was it a subtle proposition that they find someplace to better continue *this* time? Her tiny apartment, a dozen steps away up the staircase…

Her heart pounded so loudly, she wondered if Drew could hear it beating its way out of her chest. "We could—"

The ring of the phone cut off whatever Debbie might have said, and she exhaled a dizzying breath—half relief, half disappointment—as she didn't even know what her answer might have been. The machine picked up almost immediately, and Sophia's voice filled the space.

"Hey, Deb!"

And just like that, Debbie's awareness reached even further, far beyond the intimate circle she and Drew still created, beyond the kitchen and bakery, to Clearville and the outside world. A world that included loving and nosy friends and, in Drew's case, family who would have their own ideas of what her next step with Drew should be. And the step after that and the step after that, all the way to a walk down the aisle.

"Just wanted to let you know we're having a get-together this weekend and you have to come," Sophia's happy voice continued. "I want to hear all about karaoke night! Did your amazing voice knock some gorgeous guy's socks off—or maybe some other article of clothing?" Her teasing laughter ended with "Call me!"

Judging by Drew's frown, he wasn't amused. "I think I need to have a talk with Jake about my little sister. Married life is supposed to be settling her down."

"It has. Now she's trying to live vicariously through me. She's the one who sent me the info on the singles' group."

The frown darkened to a scowl. "Definitely going to have a talk."

"I doubt it will do much good. I keep telling her I'm not interested in a serious relationship, but your sister is on a mission. Ever since she got married, she's been pushing me to find someone of my own. It's that whole happy-couple-in-love thing where they want everyone else to be part of a happy couple in love, too."

"You think I haven't had my share of that? We're going to have three weddings in my family within a year. My mother would like nothing more than to see me matched up. The odd number is playing hell with her seating chart at family dinners."

Debbie could easily picture Vanessa Pirelli's exasperation. "Well, there's always Maddie."

"Ah, you're forgetting about Timmy. My niece and nephew are the cute couple at the kiddie table. I'm surprised my mom hasn't kicked me out onto the back porch."

His words brought Sophia's invitation to mind, along with memories of dozens of other Pirelli gatherings Debbie had attended over the years. They were as close to family as she had and Sophia was her best friend. If things didn't work out with Drew and if it ended up costing her that connection, that friendship…

"All of which makes this thing between us that much more complicated. If your family finds out about us—"

"I don't kiss and tell, Debbie."

"Still, it's not too late, you know."

His brow furrowed as his eyebrows pulled together. "For what?"

"To forget all of this and pretend none of it ever happened."

"Oh, yes it is. I'm going to remember your kiss for the rest of my life."

Her breath caught at his roughly murmured words. Words that said exactly what she was thinking, how she was feeling. Years from now, when she did look back, did she really only want to have kisses to remember?

Not a chance!

Drew was right. It was too late to go back. Too late to do anything but go forward.

"We're really going to do this? Have a fling?" Her face heated as she blurted out the word. It sounded so silly, but *affair* had too much of a negative ring to it, and Debbie just couldn't bring herself to ask if he wanted to have sex with her. "So…how are we going to do this?"

A sexy glint entered his gaze. "Oh, I figure the usual way."

Judging by the way he could jump-start her heart with something as simple as a smile, Debbie doubted there'd be anything *usual* about it. Still… "That's not what I meant."

"I know." That killer grin was back. "I'll take care of everything."

Not exactly an answer. At least not one she could blindly accept after taking care of herself for so long. "But—"

He silenced her with another quick kiss. "No questions or you'll ruin the surprise. Where's your sense of adventure?"

Adventure, excitement, mystery… Wasn't that exactly what she'd wished for at Darcy's bachelorette party? Drew was offering all that and more. She'd never imagined he would be the man to sweep her off her feet, but now that he had, all she could do was hold on tight and enjoy the ride…for as long as it lasted.

Chapter Eight

Drew had never claimed to be an over-the-top romantic. If he had, he was sure his former girlfriends would have quickly disabused him of that notion. In all honesty, he'd never put himself totally on the line when it came to women. Oh, sure, he'd asked out plenty, but he'd always been relatively assured of a positive response. Pursuing an uninterested woman had always struck him as a waste of time and, well, somewhat unnecessary when far more receptive members of the opposite sex could be found.

Not that Debbie was uninterested. He had no doubts about the chemistry between them. But he wanted more than a physical relationship. He wanted *Debbie* to want more than a physical relationship. More than the secret "fling" she'd proposed. Sure, he'd agreed. What red-blooded man in his right mind wouldn't? And he'd admit he wasn't ready to put his feelings on display for all of Clearville to see, especially when he knew Debbie didn't feel the same way. At least, not yet.

He'd always been one to keep his emotions close to the vest, to play things safe. But safe wouldn't do in the relationship he wanted with Debbie. He wanted the scary, reckless, no-holds-barred kind of love he used to think was out of his grasp. She'd pushed him out of his comfort zone, made him question everything he thought he knew when it came to the line between friendship and love.

After his breakup with Angie, he'd realized their relationship lacked that intrinsic connection he sensed bound his parents together. A connection Nick had found with Darcy, Jake with Sophia and Sam with Kara. He'd been ready to believe his ex was right, and he simply didn't have the necessary depth of emotion inside. But Angie had been wrong. His feelings for Debbie were beyond anything he'd felt for another woman, and going there was a giant leap for Drew, one he was ready to take.

He'd made reservations at an upscale restaurant located inside a newly built five-star hotel in Redfield. He thought he might hear from Debbie after sending her his "invitation" but she hadn't called, leaving him to wonder if she would show.

Taking a seat at the bar, he ordered a beer but barely raised the bottle for than a few swallows. His attention and his cravings were all focused on the door to the restaurant as he waited.

He hadn't realized exactly how nervous he was that Debbie might not show until the moment she walked into the restaurant. His breath escaped in a rush and he sank back against the padded back of the leather bar stool. From his vantage point in the bar, he had a perfect chance to study her unnoticed. She looked…breathtaking.

The restaurant's décor was a combination of rustic and elegant with its rough-hewn, exposed-beam ceiling and river-rock fireplace illuminated by bronze sconces and blown-glass chandeliers. Her blond hair glinted in the ambient lighting, and her soft skin was awash in a golden glow. His blood heated at just how much of that skin was revealed by her pale blue strapless dress. Black lace outlined the bodice and flirted with the hem, splitting his gaze between the curves of her breasts and shapely legs. She walked with confidence despite the spiky black heels she wore, but Drew could see a hint of nerves as she pushed her hair back behind one ear.

After thanking the hostess and taking a seat at the table, she glanced around the restaurant, but her gaze didn't travel toward his corner of bar. Seeming to come to the conclusion that she'd arrived first, Debbie glanced at the leather-bound menu. The waiter stopped by, and though Drew was too far away to hear the conversation, he watched her wave to the opposite side of the booth and figured she'd told the waiter she would wait for the rest of her party to arrive before ordering.

Her patience played into his plan perfectly. Catching the bartender's eye, he waved the younger man over. "I'd like to send a glass of champagne to the woman in the corner booth."

The bartender grinned. "Yes, sir. Anything else for you?" he asked with a nod to his lone beer.

"No, thanks," he responded.

When the bartender delivered the flute of champagne to Debbie, she took another look around the restaurant. This time, she spotted him in the bar. Her eyes lit up, and the smile she sent him hit his chest with the force of a sledgehammer.

Leaving some cash on the bar for the beer and champagne, Drew walked over to the small booth. His heart pounded, and he felt like a kid at his first school dance. It was crazy to feel so nervous about approaching someone he'd known almost his whole life. Then he caught sight of the tiny pendant she wore on a delicate gold chain around her neck, and some of the tightness in his chest eased.

She offered him a small smile so different from the bright grin she normally wore. "Hi."

"Hey. I see you got my invitation."

Her hand rose to finger the crystal slipper nestled at the hollow of her throat. "I did. Thank you. It's beautiful."

"If the glass slipper fits…"

Even in the faint lighting, he could see the blush coloring her cheeks. She glanced around the restaurant, evading his gaze, as she said, "I've never been here before. Have you?"

"No, but from what I hear, the food's great and the atmosphere is…intimate and quiet. Perfect for getting to know each other."

"Right." She gave a soft laugh. "Because you haven't known me since birth."

"I've known you as my kid sister's friend and as one of my friends. But this—this is different. And I bet there are hundreds of interesting things I don't know about you."

Doubt raised one of her eyebrows. "Like what?"

"You tell me. Tell me something I don't know about you."

"My favorite color?" she teased. "The first boy I kissed?"

"Blue," he answered. "And no, you better not tell me about the first boy you kissed, because I probably know him, and if you told me, I'd be tempted to go kick his ass."

"For a kiss that happened over a decade ago?" She laughed.

"Hey, you still remember it."

"Yes, and I remember thinking it was gross. Which is not at all what I've been thinking about more recent kisses. But I suspect that is something you already know." Their gazes caught and held as memories played between them of those stolen moments. "Now, for something you don't know..."

A door at the back of the restaurant swung open, and a waiter stepped out carrying a large tray holding steaming entrees for a nearby table. She followed the waiter's progress before looking back at Drew. "My senior year of high school, I was accepted into a culinary school in San Francisco. I wanted to study to be a chef and get a job running a kitchen in a place like this."

He'd asked for a piece of her life, something he hadn't known, but her response was more than that. It was the answer to the question he'd had, the something *more* that she'd longed for. This was the dream working in the bakery wasn't enough to fulfill.

"You're right. I had no idea."

"When I got the news, I was so excited," she said with a bittersweet smile. "My mom's cancer had been in remission for a few years, and I had such big dreams...." Her voice faded away along with her smile, and even though it happened a long time ago, Drew felt like he was watching those dreams fade away, too.

Because while he might not have known Debbie had been accepted to culinary school, he knew why she hadn't gone. Bonnie's illness had returned. And whatever hopes, whatever dreams Debbie might have had during the time when her mother's health was good had slipped away once more.

"I'm sorry, Debbie. I knew about your mom and how you'd taken over for her, but I wish I'd—I don't know... been there for you somehow."

"You were at college most of that time. Besides, there wasn't anything you could have done."

Drew's jaw tightened even though he didn't want to

admit those words hurt a little. He'd known going in that Debbie had an independent streak. And while he knew he couldn't have done anything about her mother's illness, he still could have been there for Debbie. Because that was what you did when you lo— *Cared* about someone. You stood by their side, and he refused to believe that didn't have some value.

Reaching over, he entwined his fingers with hers. "I could have held your hand, and let you know you weren't alone."

For a long time she didn't respond. But when she looked up from their joined hands, he caught the sheen of tears in her blue eyes. "I would have liked that," she said huskily.

"You know, it's not too late. If there's something else you want to do, something other than running the bakery—"

"I can't," she protested. "The bakery was my mother's dream, and with her gone…it would be like losing the only part of her I have left."

"I know how hard that would be, but what about *your* dreams?"

"I let them go a long time ago," she said, as if referring to some old toys a child had outgrown or last year's clothes that were no longer in fashion. Something meaningless and easily forgotten.

Everything inside him rebelled at the thought. Debbie was so bright, so beautiful inside and out, he couldn't stand knowing she'd given up on her dreams. On all dreams. Was that why she was willing to settle for a temporary relationship? Because she wasn't ready to believe they could have anything more?

"Debbie—"

"What about you?" she interrupted before he could say

more. "Tell me something about Drew Pirelli I don't already know."

Something she didn't know... His feelings for her tumbled around inside him, but he wasn't any more ready to put those emotions into words than Debbie was to hear them. So he settled for something far less complicated. "I'm building a house."

"You're a contractor, Drew. No real secret there."

Her teasing smile was enough to heat his blood to the point of making him want to run a finger under his collar. "No, I'm, um, building my own house."

Sitting back in her chair, she said, "You're right. I didn't know that."

"I've pretty much only told my family."

"Why?"

"I don't know. I've always felt like I put something of myself in the custom homes I build for my clients, but this is different. All the decisions, all the planning—" he gave a short laugh "—all the hard work is going into something I'm building for myself, and that's made it all much more personal. And I guess I'd rather wait and have everyone see the finished product. The hard-work part isn't always pretty."

"I think I know what you mean. Wedding cakes are the same way. Even after the crumb coat—that's a first layer of icing used to smooth out the surface of the cake— sometimes I worry that the cake's just not going to come together. That it will be lopsided or the layers will start to sag or even break. I'd never want a bride to see a cake before it's finished down to the last sugar pearl." She sipped her champagne. "So this house? Did you design it yourself?"

"I did."

"I remember at one time you were interested in studying to be an architect."

"That's where I started out. At first, everything was great. I loved the precision of designing a house. Of finding the right blend between a house that looks like a showplace but still feels like a home. Of seeing something I'd imagined take shape on paper."

"So what changed?"

"A few semesters in, I started an internship at an architecture firm. The time there gave me a really good feel for what the job would be like, just how much time would be spent behind a desk, working on blueprints or on conference calls and in planning meetings. It was enough to make me realize it wasn't what I wanted to do for the rest of my life. And it wasn't enough to just see my designs on paper. I wanted to see them come to life as I built them with my own hands."

"Judging by how successful your company is, I'd say you made the right choice."

"I'm glad business has taken off the way it has, but even if the company was struggling, I'd still know I made the right decision."

Because he'd had the opportunity to follow *his* dreams. Debbie had given up her own without complaint to care for her mother.

"I think you're incredible, you know that?"

Debbie blinked at the left-field compliment, a soft blush covering her cheeks. "I don't know about that."

"Well, there you go—something about *you* that you didn't know."

He was pretty sure she also didn't know how much he wanted to reach for her across the small table. To kiss her until they were both breathless and wanting more. But then her blush deepened even more, and he wondered if maybe she did....

The waiter cleared his throat, and Drew cursed the interruption as Debbie pulled her hand from his to smooth the napkin at her lap. After reciting the evening's specials, the young man asked, "Can I start you off with an appetizer tonight?"

"Anything sound tempting to you?" Drew asked. The only thing he was in the mood for was room service and, with any luck, breakfast in bed, but that was pushing things.

And yet Debbie seemed willing to skip some steps as she said, "You know, the best way I've found to judge a restaurant is by their desserts. What do you say to splitting the raspberry cheesecake?"

Drew grinned. "I'd say life is short. Eat dessert first."

Once the waiter left with their order, Debbie leaned closer. "Are you sure this won't spoil your appetite?"

"I don't think that's possible."

The hunger inside him wasn't the least bit satisfied by the cheesecake. Especially not when they ended up not just sharing the dessert but the same fork. When Debbie fed him a bite, all he could imagine was tasting the same sweet raspberry flavor straight from her lips.

Desire swirled between them as rich and decadent as the dessert. "I can't tell you how much I want to kiss you right now."

Her lips parted at his murmured words, drawing even more of his heated attention as she ran her tongue over the upper arch, as if already tasting him there. "Then why aren't you?"

"Because once I start, I won't want to stop."

Pulling in a deep breath that lifted her breasts against

the bodice of her dress and weakened his control even more, she said, "What if I don't want you to stop?"

"Then I'd say we should find someplace a little more private than the middle of a restaurant."

"Someplace like a hotel room?"

The key for the room he'd checked into earlier was burning a hole in his pocket. All he had to do was take Debbie's hand in his and lead her to the bank of mirrored elevator doors across the restaurant. But there was something he had to do first. Something he knew full well might ruin everything.

Sucking in a deep breath, he said, "Debbie, there's something I have to tell you. The night of Darcy's bachelorette party, I overheard your conversation with the girls."

As a kid, Debbie had fallen off her bike once and had the wind knocked out of her. She felt the same way—dizzy, panicked and unable to breathe—as Drew's words reached across the table and sucker punched her. "You heard me.... So this was all some kind of joke, then? Give poor, lonely Debbie a quick thrill, right?"

"No! No." Reaching out, Drew grasped hold of her arm when she would have otherwise jumped up and run from the booth. His grip was firm enough to let her know he didn't want her to leave yet not so tight that she'd have any trouble breaking away. But it was the warmth of his skin against hers rather than any amount of force that kept her seated. "It's not like that."

"Then tell me how it is, Drew. Tell me how you took something I said in confidence to my *friends*—" she stressed the word, making it clear she no longer considered him one of that group "—and used it to play me."

"I wasn't playing," he muttered.

"Then what were you thinking? No, let me guess. This

was all some misguided effort to save me from myself, right?" Because even as angry as she was, Debbie couldn't believe Drew would do anything purposefully cruel or hurtful. He wasn't that kind of man, and even though he hadn't been acting like himself lately, she still knew that to be true.

"You heard me say that I was looking for adventure and excitement—" her face heated at the thought of what else he'd overheard "—and you thought to yourself that couldn't possibly be good for me. Good girls are supposed to sit at home and wait for some nice boy to come calling, right? So you thought you'd step in and play superhero."

Drew's jaw tightened, but she could read the truth he was trying to hide in his dark gaze. And it hurt. So much that she felt the sting of tears at the back of her eyes. Biting down on the inside of her cheek, she willed the emotion away.

"Dammit, Debbie, will you just listen for a minute?" His shoulders rose on a deep breath as if he was struggling for calm, though why he even thought he had a right to be upset was worlds beyond her. "When I overheard you talking with Sophia and the other girls, I have to admit, I didn't like the idea of you going out and finding some stranger. The whole idea seemed—"

"Desperate?" she supplied, hopefully with enough sarcasm to mask the fact that she'd thought so herself a time or two.

"Dangerous," he argued. "The thought of you and some stranger bugged the hell out of me. And then the more I thought about it, the more the idea of you and any guy— didn't matter if it was a stranger or someone you'd known for years—started to bug me just as much."

"You're trying to tell me you were jealous," she scoffed.

"I'm trying to tell you that if any guy was going to sweep you off your feet, I wanted it to be me."

"So why not just ask me out? Why this whole ruse?"

"Because you didn't want just some everyday, average local guy to ask you out for dinner and a movie. You said so yourself."

"You really expect me to believe after all these years of *not* asking me out, all it took was overhearing that one conversation to make you suddenly realize how much you wanted to go out with me? Forgive me if I find that hard to believe." Almost as hard to believe as the jealousy undercutting his voice earlier when he spoke about the affair she'd thought she wanted to have with her tall, dark, handsome stranger.

"It wasn't just what you said. It was the way you said it."

"How? With a drunken slur?"

"You weren't drunk," Drew responded flatly. "Listening to you, I could hear the anticipation in your voice, a longing for excitement."

Her cheeks heated as her mind scrambled to think back to what else she might have said when she thought she'd been alone with her friends. "It was girl talk at a bachelorette party, Drew. Not something to take seriously and *not* something you were meant to hear."

"But I did," he argued. "And it was enough to make me realize how much excitement and mystery has been missing from my own life. Is it really so hard to believe that you're not the only one looking for something more than small-town life?"

Was it so impossible to believe? Or did she just want to believe it so much?

"Debbie—"

"I need a minute," she said as she slipped away from his touch and out of the booth.

Drew nodded and didn't try to stop her, but she read the disappointment in his gaze. He didn't think she'd be back, and as she made her escape to the restrooms, she wasn't entirely sure he was wrong. The lit sign above the exit beckoned, and she imagined herself escaping through the door and pretending this whole night had never happened.

Instead, though, she found the ladies' room and slipped inside. She'd told Drew she needed a minute, and she felt she at least owed him those sixty seconds to think about what he'd said. As she gazed into her reflection above the granite vanity, every instinct was still urging her to leave.

"You're a lucky lady, you know," a tall brunette said as she washed her hands in the sink next to Debbie.

"Excuse me?" She was hardly in the mood to engage in small talk, but the odd opening line captured her attention.

"Your boyfriend," the other woman explained. "I bumped into him at the bar earlier. I should have realized right away a guy that gorgeous had to be taken. He could barely pull his gaze away from watching the door and waiting for you to arrive." Her assessing glance traveled from Debbie's head to her toes. "You make a good-looking couple."

The woman slipped out of the restroom before Debbie had a chance to respond, but her words had already painted a picture in her mind. An image of Drew waiting for her, of him planning this night, and everything else he'd done in the past few weeks. Watching out for her at the meet and greet, showing up for karaoke night, kissing her when she looked her worst and gazing at her as if she looked her best. Did it really make a difference what had inspired Drew to arrange a night like tonight? All that really mattered was that she wanted to be with him and he wanted to be with her. . . .

Or at least he *had* wanted to be with her. Walking back

into the restaurant, she saw the booth was now empty. Had Drew left, thinking she'd changed her mind about coming back? The few bites of the cheesecake they'd shared settled like a rock in her gut. Had she blown this one chance?

But no, he wouldn't just leave. Not without making sure she was okay and likely following her back home. The gentleman in him went far too deep for him to walk out.

"Miss?"

Debbie started as their waiter appeared at her side. "Yes?"

"Your date asked me to give you this."

"Thank you." Unfolding a piece of paper, she expected to find a note. Instead the paper was folded like an envelope around a key card with a room number written inside.

No words were really necessary, were they? Drew had already stated his case. Now the choice was up to her.

And wasn't that all she'd ever really wanted? A chance to live her own life? But from the moment her mother was diagnosed with cancer, Debbie's future had been cast in stone—or shaped in a copper mold. She'd made a success out of following in her mother's footsteps, yet it had always been out of necessity and never by choice. But now Drew was giving her that choice. This next step was entirely up to her.

Did she really want to look back on tonight as something that might have been?

Denial rose up inside her, swift and sure, propelling her feet toward the elevator. No way was she letting this opportunity slip through her fingers. And no way was she going to miss this chance to get her hands on Drew. The ride up to the fifth floor seemed to take forever.

Debbie rushed toward the room, walking as fast as she could in her high heels. Her knuckles had barely rapped against the door when it was yanked open from the inside.

Moments earlier, Drew had been impeccably dressed. His pale blue dress shirt had been properly buttoned and tucked into slate-gray slacks. Now the tails hung down over his lean hips, the sleeves were pushed back to his elbows and the top buttons were undone, giving her a glimpse of the muscled chest beneath. His hair was mussed from running his fingers through it, bringing out a hint of the normally tamed curl.

The man she'd shared dessert with, who'd eaten from her fork and looked at her as if he was imagining licking the creamy cheesecake right off her, the man who normally looked so calm, so cool, so sexy was nowhere to be seen.

She liked this man even better. The relief washing over his features erased her lingering doubts. Tonight mattered to him. Almost as much as it mattered to her. "Can I come in?"

Drew stepped aside and opened the door wide. Glancing around the room, she noticed the burgundy-and-gold comforter was folded at the foot of the bed and the sheets were already turned down invitingly. Her pulse picked up its pace even as she saw the unopened bottle of champagne on ice. Her eyebrows rose as she looked back at Drew. "Pretty confident that I'd show up, weren't you?"

"Not at all," he said with a completely self-deprecating laugh. "I was hopeful that you would come and figured if you didn't, that bottle of champagne would keep me company tonight." He sobered as he crossed the room to stand in front of her. He ran his palms down her bare arms until he reached her hands and linked their fingers together. "If you're not sure about this, we can go back downstairs for dinner. We can share that champagne and then I can follow you home."

"Still trying to play the white knight, Drew?"

"It's getting harder," he confessed, and then winced at the unintended double meaning to his words.

"Then let me make it easier for you and remind you that I don't need rescuing. You don't need to save me from myself. I'm old enough to know what I want...and I want you."

Reaching up, she twined her arms around his neck and kissed him. For Debbie, it was like no time had passed between this moment of being in his arms and the last. One kiss, and she was ready for more. One touch, and she couldn't get enough.

She tasted the sweetness of raspberry and the sexiness that was pure Drew. He held her body tight to his own, leaving no doubt to how much he wanted her...wanted this. The heat pulsing through her left her weak, and when his kisses found the column of her throat, her head fell back. And when his lips traced the skin above the bodice of her dress, her bones melted like heated sugar.

He found the tab of the zipper and he made the slow slide that much more seductive by tracing his fingertips along every inch of skin he exposed. Goose bumps stood at attention, and her breasts tightened with need. She felt only a moment's hesitation as the dress fell to the floor, leaving her with nothing but her black strapless bra and matching panties. But every doubt she ever had about her hips being too round, her stomach too soft, her breasts too big was burned away by the heat of Drew's touch.

Suddenly everything that had always seemed too much or not enough was just right. A perfect fit, and Drew the perfect man...

"You are so beautiful," he breathed, and Debbie believed him. It was impossible not to when the words were spoken against her skin in a rough whisper and the hands that stripped away the last of her clothes were not quite steady.

Lifting her up in his arms like he had that night in the parking lot, he laid her down in the middle of the bed. He followed her down, but only after he'd tossed aside his own clothes, revealing a body made lean and strong by hard work—broad shoulders, muscular arms, rock-hard abs and long, powerful legs. A lock of his hair had fallen over his forehead and desire darkened his eyes to the deepest, richest chocolate.

He swallowed her gasp with his kiss at the first unrestrained contact of his body, so hard and hot above hers. She arched into his every touch—from her throat to her breast to her belly and her thighs.

It was at the same time too much and never enough, and when the rising, building pleasure broke over her, scattering pieces of her heart and soul, she knew she would never be the same.

Debbie woke in the middle of the night. She didn't need to check the clock to know sunrise was still hours away. Working at the bakery had set her internal alarm clock to a ridiculously early hour, but after so many years, she was used to it.

What she wasn't at all accustomed to was waking up in a man's arms. *Drew's* arms. He held her from behind, his body curving perfectly around hers as if the two of them were made for each other, as if they were meant to be together....

No! That was not what tonight was about. They'd agreed! *Both* of them! This was to be a fling and nothing more. And now, after one night, for her to start thinking about forever—

No! No, this wasn't happening. She wasn't falling for Drew when he'd made his own feelings more than clear.

Nah, that's just Debbie.

In high school, they'd been friends, yet in her young, foolish heart, she'd longed to be his girlfriend. Now they were lovers, and she wanted to believe making love was the same as falling in love when she was old enough to know better.

She had to get a grip on her emotions, and that wasn't about to happen while she was still wrapped in the oh-so-tempting warmth and strength of Drew's arms. She carefully pushed the covers away with one hand and tried to slip out from beneath the heavy weight of his forearm at her waist. His muscles automatically tightened, trying even in sleep to keep her close, and Debbie felt her willpower—if not her heart—fracture the tiniest bit.

It would be so easy to stay, so easy to fall even deeper, to let him get too close. Under her skin and into her heart—

Slapping a mental bandage over the break in her self-control, she eased away from Drew and out of the bed. Finding her way in the zero-dark-thirty hours of the morning was one thing. Maneuvering her way around an unfamiliar hotel room was far more difficult.

Where had all her clothes gone? Drew had been so eager to strip them away—

She slammed her mind shut on the memory, feeling her way across the plush carpet, pulling on each article of clothing as she found it—strapless bra, shoe, dress, underwear—freezing at the slightest sound coming from the bed, until she was almost fully dressed.

Almost.

What was it with her and shoes lately? She was missing a black heel, and searching for it in the darkness she couldn't help remembering the morning at Drew's house. How ruggedly handsome and yet adorable he'd looked holding the puppy in his arms. How proud and *possessive* on karaoke night when he'd called her out on wearing the shoes he'd bought to replace the ones Rain had used as a chew toy. How excited she'd been to read his invitation to meet him at the hotel and then touched to find the tiny crystal pendant inside. The pendant that had been the only thing she hadn't taken off when they made love....

There! Was that— Her fingers brushed against leather near the foot of the bed, and she almost wilted in relief as she grabbed the missing shoe. Drew's low voice came from tangled sheets, and she froze. Not an indistinct murmur, but a single word—her name. Her pulse pounded as she waited for him to ask where she was going, why she was leaving, but no other sound came from the bed. He was still asleep, her presence lingering in his dreams.... The temptation to crawl back into his arms pulled at her, her senses already craving his touch, his taste.

A shiver racked her from head to toe. She needed to go, needed time and distance to put the foolhardy dreams out of her head and out of her heart. But she couldn't escape without leaving something behind to let Drew know she was fine. That she was every bit the woman he'd overhead the night of Darcy's bachelorette party. A woman looking for adventure and excitement. A woman mature and sophisticated enough to know sex didn't equal love.

Aided by the glow of her cell phone, she found the embossed stationary and pen on the hotel room desk. After scribbling out her message, she slipped out as quietly as she could manage and closed the door behind her.

Chapter Nine

Seated on the small bistro table outside the bakery, Sophia leaned back against the white wrought iron chair and groaned dramatically around a bite of pumpkin-spice-and-chocolate-chip cupcake. "Oh, my gosh! These are *so* good. How long have you been hiding these from me?"

Debbie managed a smile and tried to smother another yawn. Her friend looked so fresh and energetic, her pregnancy glow putting Debbie to shame. She was accustomed to waking up early, but normally that meant she went to bed early, as well. Making love with Drew and spending the rest of the night alone in her bed reliving every moment she'd spent in his arms had robbed her of all but an hour or so of sleep.

She'd picked up the phone half a dozen times to call him, but she didn't know what to say. *Sorry I'm such a coward?* Or maybe *I know we agreed to a no-strings fling but after one night, I already want more?*

And she was terrified by just how *much* more. Wasn't she the same girl who didn't want to end up trapped by responsibility? Who wanted her freedom and fun? It was what she'd told her friends. It was what she'd told Drew. So why did those words sound so hollow? So…lonely?

Frustrated by the endless questions circling her mind, she'd been glad when Sophia had stopped by during her break from The Hope Chest, the antiques store just down the street from the bakery. "I haven't been hiding them. I've just added them as part of a fall menu."

"Tell me you plan to keep them on the menu. They're too good to only have for a couple of months."

"I don't know," Debbie said lightly. "Maybe what makes them so good is knowing they'll only be around for a short time."

Sophia shook her head as she dug her fork in for another bite. "No way. They're too good and too addicting to give up. Nothing else is going to compare."

And that was what she was afraid of, wasn't it? Debbie thought. Of being spoiled for life? Knowing from now on everything else would see like second best?

Pressure built in her chest, almost like feeling the need to cry, and she had to remind herself that they were only talking about *cupcakes,* for goodness' sake! She huddled deeper into the oversize cream sweater she'd grabbed before joining her friend outside in the cool, fall-scented morning.

"I left you a message and you didn't call me back," the brunette scolded once she'd finished the cupcake and reached for her herbal tea. "I hope that means you've been too busy to keep in touch with old friends," she continued with a spark in her dark eyes.

"You only left that message the day before yesterday," Debbie pointed out. But then again, a lot could happen in two days. A lot could happen in twenty-four hours. Things like meeting Sophia's brother at a hotel and spending half the night making love with him.

"Which doesn't answer the question. Did anything happen on karaoke night?"

"Karaoke night?" she echoed, feeling like so much time had already passed since then.

Sophia frowned as she crossed her arms over her pregnant belly. "You chickened out, didn't you?"

"I did not!" she protested. "I went and I even sang a couple of songs! I had a great time and—"

Drew had kissed her good-night.

She'd had a great time that night because Drew had shown up. She'd sang those songs because Drew had encouraged her. He believed in her, and that had made her want to believe in herself....

"You met someone!" Sophia exclaimed as Debbie's voice trailed off.

"I— No. No, I didn't meet anyone."

Guilt twisted Debbie's gut for not being completely honest with her friend. She'd known keeping a relationship with Drew secret would be difficult, but she hadn't thought of this part. The lying part. Although technically, she'd told the truth. She and Drew hadn't met that night. She'd known him her whole life.

But it's different now, isn't it? Different knowing him as a man instead of just as a friend....

"Gee, that's too bad," Sophia said in a voice far too innocent for Debbie to believe. "So I guess you don't have plans for tonight?"

"Why?" she asked, not bothering to hide her suspicion.

"Because," her friend drawled, "Kara's best friend, Olivia, is in town, and we're getting together for dinner. You should come with us."

The last thing Debbie wanted was to go out, but staying at home meant having nothing to do but relive each and every moment she'd spent in Drew's arms—something she'd already determined was not good for her heart. "Sure, I'll go. Sounds fun."

"Perfect! Why don't you wear the sweater you bought the last time we went shopping?"

Debbie's eyes narrowed. The sweater was the very same one she'd worn to the singles' meet and greet and was not something she would typically choose for a casual girls' night out. "Why would you want me to wear that?"

"Because you look amazing in it."

"When I bought it, you told me my boobs looked amazing in it."

"And they do!"

"And you want me to wear it tonight...why?"

"Because Sam might have run into Ryder Kincaid the other day and invited him along."

"Sophia!"

"What? Think about it. He's a Clearville guy, but he's been living in San Francisco for ten years, so you can hardly say you know everything about him."

"I know he's going through a divorce." Debbie had heard that much about the hometown boy's return.

"I know, but you keep saying that you're not interested in anything serious. I doubt he is, either."

"So you want me to be his rebound girl?"

"No, I want you to go out with a nice guy and have a good time." Heaving a sigh, Sophia leaned back in the chair and folded her arms over her round belly. "You know, for all your talk at Darcy's bachelorette party, I'm not so sure that a wild fling is really want you want at all."

Picking up her coffee, Debbie dropped her gaze to the

rich, warm brew—just the color of Drew's eyes—and tried
to tell herself her friend's words weren't all too true.

As Drew drove back home, his mood was at odds with
the crisp, clear fall afternoon. He'd known as he'd made
his way out to the job site that today was not a good day
to be working at the custom house. He was in the mood to
tear things down—preferably with his bare hands—and
not focused enough to keep his attention on the work next
on his schedule. Sure enough, by midday he had plenty to
tear down—pretty much the whole series of stairs leading
to the front deck. The stringer, steps and treads weren't up
to his standard, and he'd wasted time and material building them.

Three hours later, when he found himself snapping at
Rain as she nosed around his toolbox, chewed on an elec-
trical cord—one that thankfully wasn't plugged in—stole
his one of his leather gloves for the third time and basi-
cally acted exactly the way a puppy should act, he knew
it was time to call it a day.

Fortunately, thanks to her happy-go-lucky personality, she willingly forgave him for his bad mood and had
burned off enough energy to ride back on the seat next to
him with her head tucked against his thigh.

The hell of it was, he should have been in a great mood,
an awesome mood, after the previous night. He was more
ticked off than he wanted to admit at the way Debbie had
snuck out of the hotel room like they'd done something
wrong. It was one thing to keep their relationship secret;
treating it like something to be ashamed of was something else.

He'd agreed to the no-strings clause in their affair. He'd
orchestrated the night at the bar, doing all he could to ful-

fill her fantasy of a stranger sweeping her off her feet, because she wasn't interested in an ordinary guy like him.

But this morning, he'd thought—what? That Debbie would change her mind about what she wanted...just because he'd changed his? Maybe, Drew admitted, feeling like a fool. At the very least, he'd expected to wake with her in his arms and to spend some time together before they had to head back to Clearville and the real world Debbie found so mundane. What he sure as hell hadn't expected was to wake up alone.

And that—*sucked,* was the first word that came to mind, but it was more than that. Lifting his hand from Rain's silky fur, he rubbed at the ache in his chest. It flatout hurt, but that was his problem, wasn't it? Debbie was simply playing by the rules—a secret affair away from town, out of sight of friends and family. He was the one who already wanted to change the game.

As if sensing his mood, Rain sat up with her front paws on his denim-clad thigh and licked the side of his face. "Thanks, Rain," he said with a sigh, "but you're not the girl who can kiss it and make it better."

A few minutes later, he arrived home. With the puppy trotting at his heels, he led the way into the kitchen over to the puppy's water bowl. He'd just grabbed a beer for himself when his cell phone rang. A picture of his sister flashed across the screen. "Hey, Sophia. How's it going?"

"Drew! Oh, good. I'm so glad I caught you."

Sophia's chipper voice took him back to when they were kids, and he couldn't help using her childhood nickname as he asked, "What's up, Fifi?"

Ignoring his use of the despised nickname, she demanded, "Tell me you don't have plans for tonight."

"Why do I not have plans for tonight?"

"Because…Kara's best friend is in town, and I thought it would be fun if we all went out together."

"Forget it, Sophia," Drew protested.

"What? I've seen pictures of her and she's really pretty. And besides that, from everything Kara says, she's nice and funny and smart."

"I'm sure she is, but I'm not interested in any of your matchmaking."

"What matchmaking? It's going out with a friend of the family."

"It's a setup, and not a very good one. Doesn't she live in San Diego?"

"That doesn't mean you two can't hang out while she's here. And if things work out…"

She left the unspoken words dangling, but he refused to take the bait.

"Oh, come on! Say yes! I don't want her to feel weird being the only one there who's not part of a couple. Not that it makes you a couple if you show up. And of course Debbie and Ryder aren't a couple, either, though my fingers are crossed…."

"Wait! What did you say?" He'd almost turned out his sister's matchmaking ramblings until that last part. The untouched beer clunked against the counter. "What was that about Debbie and Ryder?"

"Sam invited him, and I thought it would be the perfect opportunity for Debbie and Ryder to get reacquainted."

"Jeez, Soph! His divorce isn't even final yet!" Yeah, like *that* was his only objection.

"No, but it will be soon, and since Debbie's not looking for anything serious, I thought he'd be someone she could go out and have a good time with."

"And Debbie—" He cleared his throat. "She agreed?"

"Sure. Just like you should agree to go out with Olivia. Come on. It'll be fun!"

"Right. Fun." Drew could think of a lot of words to describe the upcoming night, but that would not be one of them.

Debbie had tried to get out of the "date that wasn't a date," but the more she argued with Sophia, the closer she came to blurting out the truth about her and Drew. And not just the truth that they'd slept together but the whole truth—that she was terrified she was falling in love with him. And once she spoke those words out loud—even if it was just to Drew's sister—there would be no going back. Her feelings would be out there and she'd no longer be able to deny them. Not to herself and, she feared, not to Drew, either.

She had put her foot down on a few points, though. Ryder didn't need to pick her up. After all, they were meeting at the bar and grill only a block away from her shop. And Sophia would not go out of her way to force the two of them together. This was simply a group of friends having dinner together and not a date.

Sophia reluctantly agreed, but Debbie still found herself seated next to Ryder Kincaid. That she truly did believe was more by default than by design. They were simply the only two single people in the group.

While she wouldn't call the atmosphere romantic, their corner of the bar was dimly lit. Most of the illumination was provided by a few neon signs, the flash of the large-screen televisions, a chandelier made out of empty beer bottles, and the love-struck couples were taking advantage. Sophia was cuddled up to her husband, Jake, and Kara was seated next to Sam. The engaged pair had their heads bent together—maybe trying to hear each other over the mix of laughter, music and sound from the TVs, but somehow Debbie doubted the noise even penetrated their own private world. She had yet to meet Kara's friend, Olivia, and thought perhaps the other woman was running late.

"So…" Ryder began, and Debbie turned her attention to the man at her side. Wearing black trousers and a button-down black silk shirt, part of his San Francisco wardrobe no doubt, he leaned back in his chair and raised a questioning eyebrow. "How hard did Sam have to twist your arm to get you to come tonight?"

"Oh, it wasn't Sam. It was—" Debbie cut off the words, feeling her face heat as she realized what she'd just admitted.

But Ryder merely laughed, a bit of the teenager she remembered from high school coming back. He had been two grades ahead of Debbie, but she still remembered how he used to walk the halls like he owned them—star quarterback, prom king and half of Clearville High's golden couple. Ten years was a long time, and Debbie had expected him to have changed. But despite the familiar reddish-brown hair and sharp green eyes, she saw little of the carefree boy she recalled thanks to the shadows in those eyes and the new lines bracketing the sides of his mouth.

"What I meant was that Sophia is the one who invited me tonight, not Sam."

"Either way, I'm glad you came. I'd be feeling like a fifth wheel for sure in this group," he said, tilting his head toward the couple on the opposite side of the table. "And Sam was right about me needing to get out."

"What are your plans now that you've moved back?" she asked, careful not to stick her foot in her mouth again by bringing up his soon-to-be ex, Brittany, or the life he'd left behind.

"I'm going to be working with Drew Pirelli for now."

"Really? He didn't— I mean, I hadn't heard that."

"Well, it's not official since a remodeling job hasn't come up yet, but I have some appointments lined up next week for job estimates."

They spoke for a few more minutes about the remodeling jobs he would handle while Drew concentrated on the custom building when Ryder glanced over her shoulder. "There's my boss man now."

Startled, Debbie followed his gaze to the doorway leading to another area of the bar where patrons could play darts or a game of pool. Her heart skipped a beat when she saw Drew and then plummeted toward the floor as she noticed the brunette at his side.

The woman was overdressed for the small-town bar scene in a burgundy wrap dress that highlighted her slender curves. With her curly hair caught up in a messy twist and a pair of dark-framed glasses perched on her upturned nose, she had the sexy professor look down to a science. Wearing faded jeans and a navy T-shirt stretched across his wide shoulders, Drew looked that much more masculine, that much more ruggedly handsome in contrast to the beautiful woman laughing in response to his teasing smile.

"I take it that's Olivia," Debbie said, barely able to push the words past the lump in her throat.

"Yeah. Seems we're not the only setup tonight."

Catching the last bit of their conversation, Sophia leaned across the table. "I think Olivia is just perfect for Drew."

As they neared the table, Drew's gaze locked on Debbie. But while shock was still flooding her veins like ice water, he didn't appear the least bit surprised to see her seated with Ryder.

"I think they're really hitting it off. Isn't that great?" her friend gushed.

"Oh, sure. Great."

"So." Sam shot a knowing grin at his older brother. "Did Olivia kick your, um, butt in pool?"

Drew clapped him on the shoulder as he walked by. "Ran the table on me."

As Sam hooted with laughter, the brunette held up her hands. "I'm telling you guys—it's all about geometry and physics."

Debbie picked up her glass and stabbed at the ice with her straw. *More like chemistry.* She could just imagine Drew watching the slender brunette's every move as she bent over the pool table. Any guilt she felt for agreeing to go out—even as part of a group—with Ryder was quickly burned away by jealousy that Drew was there with Olivia.

"Debbie, this is my friend, Olivia Roberts. She's one of the professors at the college where I used to teach and my best friend." Kara made the introduction as Drew pulled out a chair for the other woman and then claimed the seat right next to Debbie for himself.

Leaning around Drew, the brunette greeted Debbie with a warm smile. "I've been looking forward to meeting you and stopping by your bakery. Drew says you're the best."

Debbie's gaze shot to the man next to her. He'd talked to Olivia about her?

His dark eyes captured hers, and she couldn't look away. Couldn't do anything but recall the look in those same eyes as he'd watched her come apart in his arms. "Totally addicting," he murmured now. "One taste, and I was hooked."

Hoping the sudden rush of heat to her face didn't give her away, she tore her attention away from Drew and forced herself to return Olivia's smile. "Nice to meet you."

She wasn't sure how long she sat at the table, pretending to enjoy the appetizers being passed around as she sipped at her soda. A cheer went up from the raucous crowd, but the noise, like the various games on the large-screen televisions, hardly penetrated. She could barely focus on what she and Ryder were talking about, uncertain and yet unconcerned if her responses even made sense.

All she could do was watch Drew out of the corner of her eye and wait. Wait for him to realize how pretty Olivia was. How much smarter and funnier and more interesting than Debbie was.

But as the night went on, she realized Drew had maneuvered his chair closer to hers. Close enough where his knee brushed against the outside of her thigh, robbing her of her breath while he casually participated in the conversations around them.

The first time, Debbie thought it might have been an accident. With eight people crowded around the two small tables they'd pushed together, the seating was cramped. By the fourth or fifth time, she knew he'd purposely made each move. Even through two layers of denim, she could feel the heat from his body, and it was impossible not to remember their legs tangling together with nothing in between....

Reaching for her glass, she gulped down a large swallow of diet soda, but it did little to cool last night's memories or the desire burning through her veins right then. And when Drew pressed his leg closer and *left* it there, she couldn't take it another second. After setting the glass aside, she slid her hand beneath the table and immediately realized her mistake. Because the second she touched his thigh, she was the one who couldn't pull away.

The shape and size and strength of the muscle beneath the warm, faded-to-soft denim fascinated her. Her intention to push him away evaporated as her fingertips found the inside seam of his jeans. Her nails scraped along the raised stitching as she inched higher. Drew tensed, and she thought she might have heard him mutter a curse beneath his breath before he reached down and stopped her upward progress. But instead of removing her hand, he held her palm pressed against the rock-hard muscle, teasing and tormenting them both.

Desire heated her veins, almost hot enough to burn away the reminder that Drew's "date" was sitting on his other side. *Almost.*

Some of that heat turned to anger as she pulled her hand from his grasp. "If you'll excuse me for a minute."

Her chair leg caught on Drew's as she tried to push away from the table, locking her in place. She had to wait for him to slide back before she could try to escape. She'd barely made it to her feet before he stopped her. A simple touch on her arm and *everything* stopped—her breath, her heart, the entire world around her.

She jerked back, stumbling against the stupid chair that seemed out to get her—and might have fallen if not for Drew. He caught her by the shoulders, pulling her close, just as he had in the hotel room the night before. She sucked in a quick breath, his familiar scent only adding fuel to her memories, and she could see the desire reflected in his dark eyes....

"Sorry." She forced a shaky laugh, hoping anyone watching too closely would mistake the color rushing to her face for embarrassment. "I'll be right back."

She hurried from the table, Drew's watchful gaze dogging her every step.

"Is it just me or is something up with Debbie?" Sophia asked Kara, almost shouting over the noise in the bar. Once Debbie had rushed off, Sam had challenged Jake to a game of pool, Ryder had gone for drinks and Drew had slipped way to make a phone call, leaving Sophia, Kara and Olivia alone at the table. "She hasn't been herself all evening."

"I haven't really seen her since Darcy's wedding." The blonde pulled a guilty face. "Sam and I have been busy with plans for our own wedding, and then the past few days, I've been spending time with Olivia," she added with a smile at her best friend.

Only then did Sophia notice how the brunette was eyeing them both with eyebrows raised above the frame of her glasses. "You all really don't see it?" she asked.

"See what, Liv?" Kara asked.

"It's Drew."

"Sorry…what's Drew?" Sophia asked.

Olivia gave a quiet laugh. "The *something* that's up with your friend—it's Drew."

"You mean like there's something going on between the two of them?" Sophia gave an incredulous laugh. "As much as I like the idea of my best friend getting together with my brother, I'm afraid you're wrong, Olivia. Debbie and Drew are friends—just like she's friends with Jake and Sam."

The brunette shook her head. "Debbie wasn't avoiding looking at Jake and Sam all evening. And didn't you notice the way she practically jumped out of her skin when Drew touched her? Plus, he talked about her the whole time we were playing pool. I'm telling you, something's going on."

"But if that's true," Kara asked with a frown, "why would they keep it a secret? They'd have to know how happy everyone would be to find out they're a couple."

"It's hard for you to picture the two of them as a couple because you're so used to seeing them as friends. Maybe Debbie and Drew are still getting adjusted to the idea, as well."

"I don't know," Sophia murmured doubtfully. "Debbie's been pretty adamant about not going out with Clear-ville guys."

Olivia lifted a slender shoulder. "Another reason why she might be keeping quiet about their relationship."

"If you're right—" Sophia couldn't stop the huge grin from spreading over her face. "My best friend and my brother... I've always felt that Debbie was like a big sister to me, and now we could be sisters-in-law!"

"Whoa! Moving a little fast here, don't you think?" Kara asked. "We're not even sure they're together yet."

"You're right. So what should we do?"

"Well," Olivia said wryly, "for starters, you should probably stop setting them up with other people."

Sophia threw her hands up in exasperation. "How was I supposed to know?"

Drew didn't know if anyone bought his excuse of need-ing to make a phone call seconds after Debbie disappeared toward the restrooms. Ryder had already headed to the bar, and Jake and Sam had gone off to play pool. Sophia and Kara were talking over each other in a conversation that skipped from baby names to bridesmaids' dresses to nursery decorations and honeymoon locations so quickly, even trying his hardest not to listen made his head swim. But Olivia had given him a studied glance as he pushed away from the table—like he was some kind of equation she was trying to solve.

Good luck with that, he thought with a snort. He couldn't even figure out what he was thinking or feeling or doing from one second to the next. He still couldn't believe he'd let Sophia set him up, even if he had his own reasons for showing up at the bar that night.

He had to admit, though, that Sophia had been right about Olivia. She really was pretty. Behind the dark-framed glasses, her eyes were a rich, warm brown, and she had a sprinkling of freckles like gold dust across her upturned nose and fair cheeks. "First Sam and now you," she had commented after Sophia made the introduction. "I can see why a single woman would consider moving to your hometown."

She was smart and funny and charming. But as cute as her upturned nose was, it didn't crinkle when she smiled. And as much as he liked the freckles, somehow he'd missed the sight of a dimple in her cheek when she laughed, and her eyes couldn't nail him to the spot with just a glance because they were brown. Brown and not blue.

Thankfully, Olivia was savvy enough to realize his head—not to mention his heart—wasn't in the game. Hadn't stopped her from wiping the floor with him in pool, but he figured he'd deserved that.

The music and laughter faded a little as he stepped into the narrow hallway leading to the restrooms and the door to the back parking lot. He felt like a stalker, lurking outside the women's restroom. More so when Debbie stepped into the darkened hall and gave a startled gasp. "Drew!" Her blue eyes grew even wider when he took her hand and led the way out back. "What are you doing?"

The cool night air and silence was a relief from the crowded bar, and he pulled in a deep breath. A few lights along the back of the lot illuminated the cars, but moonlight provided most of the glow. Debbie's eyes glittered like jewels and her hair looked more silver than gold, but still as soft as ever cascading over her shoulders. She hadn't dressed up for the evening—something that pleased him probably more than it should—but she still looked amazing to him in faded jeans and a long-sleeved turquoise sweater.

"I wanted to talk to you. To see if you're okay."

He'd never had a one-night stand and wasn't the type

of guy to sleep with a woman and then walk away without a backward glance. Not that he had been the one to walk away.

Debbie had.

She reacted to his concern as if he'd accused her of some kind of weakness, drawing her shoulders back and lifting her head. "I'm fine. I just—didn't expect to see you until—"

"Next week," he finished, trying to ignore the annoyance still buzzing like a relentless mosquito inside him at the memory of the note she'd left behind.

She cleared her throat. "Right. Next week. But since you're here, there are some things we didn't have a chance to talk about after last night."

"The way I remember it, we didn't talk at all."

Her gaze quickly cut away from his. Was she simply embarrassed, or could he hope that she regretted sneaking out the way she had? "Yes, well, I didn't think this conversation would be necessary, but now—" She waved a hand in an all-encompassing gesture. "Obviously it is."

Since Drew didn't find anything obvious about the whole conversation, he asked, "What exactly is it that we need to talk about?"

Debbie took a deep breath. "Seeing other people."

Her words his like a sucker punch to his gut. That was what Debbie wanted to discuss? She wanted to see other people? He'd convinced himself she wasn't really interested in Ryder. That she couldn't be—not after the night the two of them had shared. It was the only way he'd kept from decking the guy when he'd seen his newest employee sitting next to Debbie.

Had he just been fooling himself in thinking the date had been a harmless setup by his sister? Fooling himself in thinking that giving Debbie what she wanted—a no-strings affair—would eventually lead her to realize she wanted more?

"If this is going to work," she continued, "we need to have some—ground rules."

Rules. Probably something along the line of Drew *not* punching the other guy in the face. Uncurling the fists he'd unconsciously made, he said, "Go on."

"As long as we're—together, I expect us to be monogamous." Finishing in a rush, she added, "I don't see how this can work if that's going to be a problem for you."

Relief washed over him, draining away the tension before a feeling of irritation crept in. "For me? You're the one bringing up the idea of seeing other people in the first place!"

"And you're the one who's here with Olivia!" she shot back.

Crossing his arms over his chest, he met her angry gaze and tried to hide a smile. If she was as pissed off about seeing him with Olivia as he'd been about seeing *her* with Ryder—somehow that made his own anger and jealousy drain away. Looked as though Debbie was going to be the first to tie some strings around their no-strings affair. That worked perfectly for Drew, who already felt so tangled up in knots about the woman in front of him he didn't think he'd ever work his way free.

Still, he had to point out, "The chair next to you wasn't exactly empty, sweetheart."

She had the grace to duck her head, and some of the tension eased from her shoulders. "It's not like I'm here with Ryder. I'd already agreed to go out tonight before your sister sprung the news on me that he'd be here, too."

"I know. She set both of us up."

"So you already knew I'd be here tonight?"

"Why do you think I came? And don't say because of

Olivia. Nice as she is, she's not the woman I want, and I don't want to wait until next weekend to have you in my arms again."

For a split second, he thought she might argue, but instead she breathlessly asked, "What about your family?"

"We'll tell them we both have early mornings and need to head out."

When they went back inside, though, their excuses were barely needed. Only Kara and Sophia were still sitting at the table, and Debbie had just made note of the time when Sophia exclaimed, "Oh, you're right! It is getting late, isn't it? We're all about ready to head out, too." She glanced over at Kara, who quickly nodded in agreement as Sophia reached for her purse beneath the table. "Drew, you wouldn't mind walking Debbie home, would you?"

Narrowing his eyes, he looked at his sister, who gazed back—all wide-eyed and innocent. *Yeah, right...* Still, he knew better than to look a perfect excuse in the mouth. "Of course I will."

"Um, what about—" Debbie glanced toward Ryder's empty chair.

"Olivia and Ryder challenged Jake and Sam to one last game of pool before we go," Kara explained.

"Don't worry. We'll let them know you two had to head out early."

"Thanks, Sophia."

"Oh, sure!" His little sister flashed a wink his way. "Told you tonight would be fun."

He had a feeling Sophia was enjoying herself a little *too* much. Still, if she had figured out what was going on between him and Debbie, it felt good to know she was on his side. Leaning down, he brushed a kiss across her forehead. "Thanks again."

Catching his arm before he could pull away, she was

still smiling as she said, "She's my best friend. Break her heart, and I break you."

He managed a smile of his own, his teasing words all too serious as he asked, "What happens if she breaks mine?"

Chapter Ten

Debbie cut the engine on her small VW but hesitated in getting out of the car and entering the Pirellis' large farmhouse. Terra-cotta flowerpots filled with bright-faced pansies and purple snapdragons marked each step on the way up to the wraparound porch, and a fall-inspired wreath made of silk mums and decorated with miniature pumpkins added a splash of red and gold and orange to the front door. The place looked as homey and welcoming as ever, and it was ridiculous to feel nervous.

She couldn't count the number of times she'd been invited over for dinners, birthdays and holidays. But tonight was different. Tonight she worried Drew's parents were going to take one look at her and know what had happened between her and their middle son at the hotel in Redfield… and at her place the weekend before.

When she'd entered into this secret affair with Drew, she'd never imagined inviting him back to her apartment.

Bad enough he already haunted her thoughts when she lay in her bed alone. How would she ever sleep again once she'd experienced sleeping there with him beside her? But from the moment Drew admitted he couldn't wait to have her in his arms again, she hadn't been thinking.

The walk from the bar had seemed to take forever, and the back door of the bakery had barely closed before Drew reached for her. Unlike at the hotel when he'd seduced and romanced her, giving, taking and teasing, that night his kisses had demanded. He'd left her desperate and wanting, begging for more, and she'd been the one to lead them to the narrow staircase to her small apartment. Their clothes had littered every other step along the way, and they'd barely made it to the bed before he was inside her....

She didn't know how she could look at him without every heated memory reflecting on her face, and she already regretted agreeing to come. Sophia had been way too persuasive and she— Well, she hadn't been able to think of an adequate excuse for skipping—other than blurting out the news that she was sleeping with her friend's brother.

So now she was sitting in her car in front of Drew's parents' house, feeling as guilty and self-conscious as if the two of them had been caught making out in the backseat.

"You're being ridiculous," she scolded herself. And despite her fears, a glance in the rearview mirror proved that her attraction to Drew wasn't written all over her face.

She could do this.

"Debbie! Good, you're here!" Sophia greeted her as she opened the front door to Debbie's knock. "And you brought dessert!"

"What else?" she asked somewhat wryly as she balanced the cake box in one hand.

"I'll take this to the kitchen. We're about ready to eat."

"Am I late?" she asked as Sophia led the way through

the living room that held the same slightly worn and comfortable couches and chairs from her last visit, but the family portrait above the fireplace was new. The previous photo had been taken a few years ago. The updated one included the newest members of the family—Jake, Darcy, Kara and Sam's son, Timmy.

Drew's image smiled out from behind the glass, and Debbie wondered if it was only her imagination that his expression seemed a little wry. *Last man standing.* The picture seemed to emphasize the teasing comment she'd heard at Nick's wedding as Drew was the only unattached member of his family.

Saving the best for last, she thought with a small smile of her own.

"No, you're right on time. But you know how it is around here." Sophia rolled her eyes. "The guys are always starving."

With a nod toward the formal dining room, Sophia said, "Go ahead and have a seat. My mom's got everything under control in the kitchen."

"Are you sure I can't help?"

Vanessa Pirelli stepped through the swinging door from the kitchen in time to hear Debbie's question. She held a large pan of bubbling, mouthwatering lasagna in her oven-mitted hands. The scent of oregano, garlic, basil, rich tomato sauce and decadent cheese filled the air. "Sophia's right. I've got this, and you know what they say about too many cooks spoiling the lasagna."

"I don't think anything could spoil your lasagna, Vanessa."

"Hmm, except maybe your chocolate cake. This group would just as soon eat dessert first."

On those words, an echo from the night at the hotel, Debbie stepped into the dining room. Her gaze immediately locked on Drew. He was helping his dad move dishes around on the table—one holding steaming garlic bread, another a tossed salad and smaller bowls filled with dressing, croutons and grated parmesan cheese—to make way for the main dish. At his mother's statement, he looked up and the subtle grin he shot her was enough to weaken her knees.

"Have a seat, Debbie. There's a spot for you right beside Drew."

He rolled his eyes at his mother's pleased statement even as he pulled out the chair. Debbie fought a smile and shot him a warning look as she sat down. His grin only widened in response. Bending low as she slid her chair closer to the table, he whispered, "Try to keep your hands to yourself this time."

"You started it," she retorted with a benign grin.

A shiver raced down her spine when his heated, sidelong glance reminded her just how well he'd finished what he'd started, too.

Pirelli family dinners had always been crowded, noisy affairs, and that was before adding Jake, Darcy, Kara and Timmy to the mix. The result was a constant passing of food and a half a dozen conversations taking place at once. It was completely different from the quiet meals she used to share with her mother at their round, two-person table. As much as she missed her mother, Debbie loved the laughter and chaos of the big group.

Vince Pirelli, an older, heavier version of his dark-haired sons, kept up a running dialogue about sports with the guys while fielding "guess what, Grandpa?" questions from Timmy, most of which revolved around the boy's love of dinosaurs and his excitement over his Halloween costume and trick-or-treating the next weekend.

Vanessa, meanwhile, engaged the rest of the table with

updates on out-of-town relatives as well as local news. "I heard Anne Novak is moving to Colorado to be with her family," she said to Debbie as she passed the garlic bread.

Debbie nodded. Anne had been her "neighbor" for the past few years, running a used bookstore in the space beside the bakery. "She's so excited to be closer to her grandkids."

"I'm sure she is. Still, I know you're going to miss her."

"I will. She's been a good friend, and I enjoyed having the bookstore next door. I hope another business moves in soon."

"Oh, wouldn't it be great if a clothing boutique moved in?" Darcy asked.

"Right. Because it's not like you don't already have enough clothes," Nick said to his fashionable wife.

"Daddy, you can never have enough clothes," his eight-year-old daughter, Maddie, chimed in.

The laugher almost drowned out Nick's groan.

After a few minutes of the women debating what other new businesses they'd like to see, Drew said, "I think you should take over the space, Debbie."

Barely managing to swallow a bite of lasagna without choking, she sputtered, "Me?"

"Sure. Think of how you could branch out and do so much more with the extra space—add some sandwiches and salads to the menu. You could turn the bakery into a café."

Debbie caught her breath at the unexpected suggestion. Pressure built in her chest at his words, along with the sting of tears behind her eyes, and she didn't even know why. Okay, so years ago she'd had hopes of going to culinary school and opening a restaurant. For Drew to bring up that long-denied dream now, well, it hurt.

She felt as though he'd dismissed the past four years

she'd spent working to make the bakery a success. The hard work she'd done to *forget* that she'd once wanted something bigger than the bakery.... But that was before the heartbreaking reality of her mother's illness had crashed down on the both of them.

Her voice sharpened by the jagged memories, she echoed, "More than the bakery? Because you don't think that's enough?"

His eyebrows rose slightly at her tone, but his voice was calm as he asked, "I don't know, Debbie. Is it?"

It had to be enough, because what else was there? She couldn't turn her back on the bakery any more than she could have turned her back on her mother to follow her own dreams.

"The bakery is more than enough to keep me busy, and speaking of which—" she pushed back her chair and glanced around the table "—is everyone ready for dessert? I brought everyone's favorite—double chocolate!"

A loud cheer went up, lead mostly by Sam's four-year-old, Timmy, who started a chant of, "Cake, cake, cake!"

Standing, she turned toward the kitchen, relief inching through her as she thought she might make good on her escape. But Drew, ever the gentleman, stood as well, effectively blocking her exit.

"Debbie..." He placed a hand on her arm, and something about the look in his dark eyes grabbed hold of her heart and wouldn't let go....

But she still pulled away from his touch and brightly promised, "I'll be right back with that cake!"

"So was it my imagination, or did I see some sparks flying?" Sam asked Drew. After dinner and dessert, the guys had split off on one side of the living room with the women on the other as Darcy regaled them with her tales of love at first sight—for every shoe store and ultrachic boutique she'd set foot in during the trip to Paris. She'd also brought back gifts for her friends, and they were all currently oohing and aahing over the silver frame she'd given to Sophia with her soon-to-arrive baby in mind.

"Sparks?" Drew echoed, his gaze automatically shifting toward Debbie. She was laughing at Darcy's effusive storytelling, looking happy and relaxed with no sign of the tension twisting between them earlier.

It had been a mistake to push. He'd known that as soon as he'd opened his mouth. Debbie had a stubborn streak to go along with her independence, and there was no way he could force her in a direction she didn't want to go. Which should have kept him from talking to her in front of his entire family. He didn't know why he'd tried except that it still bothered him that he'd never questioned her reasons for not changing the bakery. Never wondered if stepping into her mother's footsteps was enough to make her happy.

"You and Olivia."

Drew barely stopped himself from repeating the woman's name. If he kept mindlessly echoing everything his brothers said, they were bound to notice. But his distraction wasn't thanks to Kara's best friend.

"Sam says you went to dinner together when she was here in town."

Olivia had gone back to San Diego, but Nick was clearly getting caught up on what had been happening while he was on his honeymoon. "A whole group of us went out to dinner. It wasn't a date."

"It could have been if you'd ask her out after that," Sam pointed out. "I gotta say, no one thought you'd be the last of us to get married."

"That's because no one ever thought you'd get married at all."

"All it took was meeting the right girl." Sam's expression softened as he glanced across the room at his fiancée.

It still felt weird to see his little brother so in love, and a hell of a lot more like jealousy than Drew wanted to admit. He might have thought Sam, who had a reputation for avoiding commitment and never taking life too seriously, would have some major doubts about settling down with one woman for the rest of his life. But Sam being Sam, he seemed to take the upcoming wedding as one big adventure, with his typical exuberance and good humor.

He looked over at Nick. "When you know, you know. Right, Nick?"

"Right, Sam," he echoed with a grin. He sobered slightly as he met Drew's gaze. "It's like suddenly your eyes are open and you realize the woman you've been waiting for your whole life is standing right in front of you. And you know."

Drew swallowed as his brother's soft-spoken statement lodged in his chest. The words fit Debbie perfectly. He'd known her her whole life and that entire time, she'd been right there. Right in front of him, and all he had to do was open his eyes.

He'd always cared for Debbie, but his feelings were— different now. And not just because of the sex. He'd been in enough relationships to know that sex didn't necessarily lead to love. More often than not, the opposite was true. Sex came first and nothing followed. Making love with Debbie had made him realize just how empty those previous relationships had been.

"I'll tell you what I know," he ground out once he was sure he could speak around the lump in his throat. "Olivia's a great girl, but she's not the one. Just as well, since I'm not looking to settle down."

His brothers exchanged a look and then burst into laughter. He couldn't remember the last time he'd made them laugh so hard…especially when he hadn't said anything so damn funny. "What?" he demanded, irritated by their reaction and just irritated in general.

"Dude, you are so ready to settle down. You were like born ready."

Nick nodded his agreement. "Just look at the house you're building."

"It's an investment," Drew argued, wondering if he could sound any more lame.

"It's a home for a family," his older brother stressed.

"That—" Sam gave a soft snort "—or a really big doghouse."

"Rain will have plenty of room to roam," Nick agreed with a smug smile, clearly still feeling he'd somehow conned Drew into taking the puppy off his hands.

"Think whatever you want," he said testily, "but the only walk I'm going to be taking down the aisle is as your best man, Sam."

Nick's gaze swung toward their younger brother. "You told me I was going to be best man."

"He's just saying that. I haven't decided yet. You're both my brothers." Sam's wide shoulders lifted in a shrug. "How am I supposed to choose?"

"Easy. You pick me. I'm the oldest anyway."

"What? And that means you automatically get to be my best man or just that you automatically get to tell me what to do?"

"Both!"

Leaving them to the argument that had been going on since the minute Sam had gotten engaged, Drew used the opportunity to slip away. He was heading toward the kitchen when another outburst caught his attention—this time from the female corner of the living room.

A catcall and a few whoops went up as Debbie held a clinging black negligee against her body. Drew's mouth went dry. It didn't matter that the only thing he could see through the sheer lace was the cream-colored sweater and floral leggings she'd been wearing all evening. He knew what was beneath those leggings and that sweater and could imagine what her creamy skin would look like draped in black lace as easily as he could picture himself slowly stripping the negligee away from her gorgeous curves.

"As soon as I saw that nightgown, I thought of our conversation the night of my bachelorette party and knew I had to get for you…just in case."

Just in case Debbie found a handsome stranger to sweep her off her feet. Darcy might not have known Drew had overheard that conversation, but Debbie did. He waited, caught in a mix of anticipation and dread, for her blue eyes to swing his way. And when they did—

Jerking his gaze away, he stalked off into his parents' kitchen. He doubted his mom had any hard liquor on hand, but maybe he could stick his head in the freezer and at least cool off part of his body. Even if it wasn't the half ready to explode. He'd downed a glass of ice water and was going back for a refill when the door behind him swung open and Debbie stepped inside. Just like that his heart rate jumped into high gear and his blood heated. At least she'd left the nightgown back in the living room.

"Drew—"

"Debbie—"

They both broke off with a short laugh, some of the tension easing as they spoke at the same time. "Ladies first."

"I'm sorry about snapping at you earlier," she blurted out. "It's been a long time since I seriously thought about doing something other than running the bakery. I never told anyone about applying to culinary school. No one except you, that is."

"You didn't tell Bonnie?" The two of them had been so close, Drew couldn't imagine Debbie keeping such a big secret from her mother.

"When I first applied, I didn't really think I'd get in."

"But once you did—"

"Once I did, my mom's cancer had already come back. Telling her about the school, about what I was giving up to stay with her, would have only made her feel bad."

"Just like me bringing it up again made you feel bad," he guessed.

Debbie ducked her head, but not before he saw the lingering hurt shining in her eyes. Swearing beneath his breath at his own stupidity, he pulled her into his arms and felt the rest of the tension leave his body when she nestled willingly into his chest.

"I'm sorry, sweetheart. And I swear that wasn't my intention. I just thought this might be an opportunity for you to branch out, to go after what you really want." He hated the idea of her settling for less. She deserved a career that left her fulfilled instead of empty. And an open, honest relationship instead of one she felt the need to hide.

Or was that just what *he* wanted?

"I know, and that's why I'm sorry for reacting the way I did. But I'm finally at a point where I can relax a little. Where I have a bit of freedom to go out and have a good time and—"

"Find some tall, dark stranger to have a secret fling with?" Drew filled in.

Still holding her, his chin resting against the softness of her blond hair, he could feel as well as hear her laughter. The vibrations settled into his chest, into his heart, the same way Debbie had.

"Some tall, dark, *handsome* stranger," she stressed. "I don't want to give that up...." Lifting her head, she met his gaze as she hesitantly asked, "Do you?"

"Give it up? Not a chance." He wanted more, not less. "I just don't see why it has to be one or the other."

"Because that's the way it's always been," Debbie confessed. "The bakery comes first and everything else a distant or nonexistent second. And sometimes I get so tired of it that I just want to quit, but how do you quit when you're the boss and it's your business and my mom— She would be so disappointed in me if she knew I felt this way."

"I think you're right."

His words stabbed at her, and her startled gaze flew to his. "That's not what you're supposed to say. You're supposed to tell me I'm wrong and my mother would never hate for me for feeling like this."

"Okay, *now* you're wrong. Your mother would never hate you, but I do think she'd be disappointed that you aren't following your own dreams. That you aren't doing what *you* love. I can't imagine that she would have left you the bakery if she didn't think you'd be happy."

"*She* was," Debbie admitted. "She was so happy to run the bakery, and sometimes I wonder what's wrong with me that it's not enough...that I want more. But you already figured that out, didn't you? And I jumped all over you because just hearing you suggest it made me feel so guilty."

"There's nothing wrong with you, and there's nothing wrong with wanting more. With wanting...everything."

Gazing into his dark eyes, Debbie almost forgot to breathe. She could so easily get lost in the caring and compassion she saw there. In the undefined *everything* he was promising. "I, um, do want to make some changes at the bakery. Now that I've hired Kayla, it's given me time to focus on expanding the menu—"

"Like with the fall cupcakes," he said, the deepening of his voice telling her he was remembering more than tasting the pumpkin spice and chocolate cakes.

"Exactly. And I—I've done some more promotion for wedding cakes. It's not totally new for me. I've made several over the years, but just locally for friends and acquaintances. It's never been a big part of the business."

"Everyone raved about the cakes you made for Darcy and Nick and for Sophia and Jake."

"Well, I don't know that everyone did—"

"Then you just didn't hear them, because believe me, sweetheart, people couldn't stop talking about how beautiful they looked and how great they tasted—kind of like the woman who made them."

Sputtering a laugh, Debbie said, "Well, I hope you're right—about the cakes, at least. I asked Darcy and Nick's photographer to take some extra shots of the wedding cake. As soon as I get those back I'm going to redesign my website with a page just for wedding cakes, as well as doing some advertising in bridal magazines. I'm kind of excited to see what the response might be." As she said the words, Debbie realized it was true. "It's a part of the bakery that could be all mine, you know?"

"Yeah, I get that. It's like the house I'm building. I work just as hard and pay just as much attention to detail on every house, but it still feels different knowing this one is going to be my own."

The sound of voices from the living room carried into the kitchen. "What? I'm just going for drinks."

The door swung open, but not before Debbie had a split second to step out of Drew's embrace. The platter of leftover cake sitting on the kitchen island caught her attention, and by the time Sam stepped inside with Sophia following close on his heels, she was calmly slicing the dessert. "I'm cutting the leftovers into smaller pieces. Do you both want to take some home?"

"Probably shouldn't." Sophia placed her hands on her expanding stomach. "Jake will eat it all and yet I'll be the one to end up gaining weight."

"Are you kidding?" Sam asked. "Timmy would eat cake for breakfast if we let him. Drew, pass me a couple of beers, will you?"

As he tossed Sam the cans, Sophia looked from Drew to Debbie and back again. "So what were you two talking about in here?"

"My new house," he answered before Debbie could even come up with an excuse.

"It's going to be amazing, Debbie. You should see it—" Her dark eyes lit suddenly. "In fact, that's a great idea! Drew, you should take Debbie out there and give her a tour."

"Oh, I don't know, Sophia," Debbie protested, remembering his comment that he wanted the house finished before showing off the place.

But he was already pulling his keys from the pocket of his jeans. "Let's go."

Chapter Eleven

"Are you sure you don't mind taking me to see the house?" Debbie asked as Drew climbed behind the wheel. "I remember what you said about wanting to show off the finished product."

"I figured you could maybe use a break from my family." Drew glanced over at her as he guided the oversize SUV away from the Pirellis' home.

"Are you kidding? I love your family."

"Well, then, maybe I'm the one who needed a break from them," he said wryly. "Especially if it means being alone with you."

A small shiver raced through her at his words, and she grinned as he reached over and took her hand. Too bad the cab had bucket seats with a gearshift preventing her from sliding up against him. Instead she had to settle for twining her fingers through his and feeling the pressure of his knuckles against her leg.

For a few minutes, they sat in easy silence, driving

down the highway cutting through the towering pines, until Debbie asked, "What were you, Sam and Nick talking about earlier? It looked pretty serious."

His broad shoulder lifted in a shrug. "Usual stupid stuff. Arguing over who would be Sam's best man."

She wasn't sure why, but she didn't think his explanation was 100 percent true. "You're lucky, you know, and I've always been a little envious."

"Why? Do you want to be Sam's best man?"

"Very funny. What I meant is that growing up I used to wish I had brothers and sisters. Not that I told my mom that. She wanted more kids, but it wasn't meant to be."

"I always liked your mom. I remember her sneaking me and my brothers cookies while my parents pretended not to notice. The thought that we were getting away with something made those bite-size treats taste even better."

"Forbidden fruit," she teased even as she recalled her conversation with Sophia at the bakery the other day. Was the newness and the secrecy of her relationship with Drew what made it so sweet? she wondered. But then Drew moved his thumb, stroking her skin through the thin fabric of her leggings, and she couldn't imagine the rush of desire ever growing old. Couldn't imagine her feelings ever fading.

Drew pulled the SUV off the paved road and slowed to a bumpy crawl over a long, graded driveway. As they rounded a curve, Debbie glanced through the front windshield. "Oh, Drew."

When he climbed from the truck and came around to open her door, she slid from the passenger seat and got an even better look at the house he'd built. Nestled in a wooded grove, the towering pines and the fading rays of sunset were the perfect back for the beautiful house. Even though the raw, unfinished wood was still exposed, the solid shape and style of the house was apparent. The front had a traditional Craftsman porch and entry with two columns on either side of the steps. But the house spread out, far larger than the typical turn-of-the-century homes.

"It doesn't look like much yet. The siding still needs to go up and eventually the base of the columns will be covered by stone veneer. I'm planning to stain the porch and stairs to match," he said as he led the way up those same stairs.

"It's incredible," she breathed as he opened the door and ushered her inside.

"With the exposed wires and piping, sometimes it can be hard to imagine what it will look like with actual walls and floors made of something other than concrete."

Despite the typical construction dust and debris, Debbie didn't have any trouble at all picturing the home when it was finished. The foyer opened into a large great room. The far wall was almost all windows, giving a view of the mountains and trees backed up to the property. Room had been left for a large deck, and she could almost smell the scent of grilled burgers filling the air along with the sound of laughter as the Pirellis gathered in Drew's backyard.

To the right of the living room was the kitchen, a huge expanse, empty now but with plenty of room for state-of-the-art appliances. Debbie could see the outline on the bare floors, marking the location of a large center island. The open floor plan would make it possible for whoever was in the kitchen to still interact with family and guests. A formal dining room was framed in on the other side of the great room, but Debbie knew most meals would be shared around the island. Another room with the same view of the mountains was reserved for Drew's study. And then he showed her the bedrooms.

Lots of bedrooms.

"This is really a big house," she said as they stood in one of the secondary bedrooms. A child's bedroom—one that would start out as a nursery and then grow from there along with the child who slept within its walls.

Drew's child. A quietly serious, dark-haired, dark-eyed boy. Or maybe a sweetly shy daughter who would have her daddy wrapped around her little finger. She could almost hear the childish laughter filling the room.

"I figured if I was going to go through all the work of building my own place, it should include everything I want."

Everything he wanted... He'd told her that he, too, was looking for adventure and excitement when they started out on their affair, but what was that saying about actions speaking louder than words? This house, this home Drew was building with his own hands, this was the reality he truly wanted. A wife, kids, a family to go along with the dog he already owned.

He'd encouraged her to go after her dreams, but how was she supposed to encourage him to go after his when it meant letting him go? And not just losing what they had, but losing him to another woman?

The ache in her chest grew until she could barely breathe. She turned away from the room, from the image of the child who would one day sleep inside it, but Drew was right there. Waiting...watching... His gaze caught hers and something...happened. Those dreams of the future, Drew's dreams, were written in clear detail in the longing on his handsome face. The wife, the kids, the family. Only suddenly Debbie saw herself in the reflection of his dark eyes. Saw herself as his wife, his children as her children, his family as her family....

And the feeling that surrounded her wasn't one of pressure, of responsibility closing in and trapping her on every side. Instead the embrace was filled with hope, with possibility and with love.

"Follow me home?" Debbie asked as Drew pulled his SUV next to her small VW parked in his parents' driveway. Her heart was pounding as if she was asking Drew to make love to her the first time. She couldn't pretend tonight wouldn't be different. Admitting how she felt—even just to herself—would only leave her heart that much more open to Drew. She'd no longer be able to hide behind the pretense that their relationship was some kind of no-strings affair.

But looking at the heat in Drew's eyes, she couldn't help wondering if the only one she'd been fooling was herself....

"I might just beat you there."

Laughing, she was reaching for her purse when her cell phone rang. She didn't recognize the number but swiped the screen to accept the call. "Hello?"

"Debbie, this is Andrea Collins."

"Andrea, hello." Debbie hoped her voice didn't reveal her surprise. Andrea was the town's Realtor, and while Debbie knew the older woman by sight and reputation, they weren't close enough to have exchanged cell phone numbers. "How are you?"

"How am I? I'm desperate, that's how I am. I need your help."

"Help with what?" Catching her side of the conversation, Drew raised his eyebrows, but Debbie could only shrug.

"Saving a wedding and the lives of my unborn grandchildren."

"Um, okay. Wow. How can I help with that?"

"My lovely daughter is getting married. This weekend. And her husband-to-be, man that he is, gladly left all the details up to her. 'It's your day, dear. Whatever makes you happy makes me happy.'" Andrea quoted her future son-in-law's voice with a heavy dose of sarcasm. "Yeah, right."

"I take it he's not happy?"

"No, he is not. Evidently, he's allergic. To strawberries—as is half of his entire, anaphylactic family."

Starting to get a feel for where the conversation was going, Debbie said, "Let me guess. Your daughter's wedding cake has strawberries on it?"

"On it. In it. With berries carved into tiny flowers topping the whole gorgeous, inedible thing."

"Did you contact the bakery?"

"Oh, sure, as soon as we realized the problem. But it's too late. They book their weddings months in advance, and while they are very sorry for our problem, it's very much our problem and they have no solution to offer. Debbie, please, I am desperate. Caroline is my only child and she is thirty-five years old. My window of opportunity for becoming a grandmother is closing fast, and I will not have it slam shut because of a food allergy."

"I doubt your daughter and her fiancé would call off the wedding just because of the cake."

"You'd be surprised. Caroline has a serious case of cold feet. She's looking at any negative as a sign that she's not supposed to go through with this wedding, even though her fiancé, despite his allergies, is an amazing man who adores her. Please, Debbie. I tried telling my daughter we could get a cake from the grocery store, and I thought she was going to pass out. You are my last hope. I heard all about the cake you made for Nick and Darcy's wedding. I know you can do this."

After asking Andrea to send her a photo of the type

of cake her daughter had in mind, Debbie explained the trouble to Drew. "Jeez, I'm not sure who I feel more sorry for," he said, "Caroline, her fiancé or Andrea."

"I can't believe Caroline's fiancé didn't tell her about his allergy."

"Ah, give the poor guy a break. His mind was probably focused on the honeymoon."

"Not sure it was his mind," Debbie muttered, but Drew only grinned in response. He climbed from the SUV and opened the door for her. A second later, her phone beeped and an image of the cake glowed on the screen.

"Oh, wow." She'd seen her share of amazing cakes—even made a few herself—but the photo was of a masterpiece. The graduated round layers were covered in white fondant and decorated with a diamond-shaped quilted pattern. Small gold sugar pearls dotted each point, and the dreaded, delicately carved strawberries waterfalled from one level to the next. And if all that wasn't challenging enough, the tiers didn't stack one on top of the other. Instead they were offset, almost defying gravity, with an impressive height.

Even Drew let out a low whistle. "That is some cake."

"I don't think I can do this. I mean, if I had *days,* maybe, but by tomorrow? I don't know… And besides, we have… plans."

"It's only one weekend, Debbie."

"But that's just it. It's not. It's been every weekend for the past ten years," she said with a sigh. "The bakery comes first and everything else is second."

"It's not the same thing. This is your chance, sweetheart. You told me you wanted wedding cakes to be a bigger part of the business, and you know Andrea Collins. She has connections all over the place. You do this for her, and she'll be all the advertising you need."

"Yeah, and if I blow it—"

"You can do this." Lifting her hand, he held the screen and the image of the cake in front of her. "You can do *this*."

"Drew…you don't understand. I've never made a cake like that before. The cakes I've made have always stacked on top of each other with dowels or decorative pillars to support the layers above. This—this is—"

"It's a spiral staircase." He pointed to the cake. "There's a center column, just like on a staircase, and each layer of cake is like one of the treads. As long as the column is solid and secure to the base, it'll support the treads with no problem. Or in this case, the layers of cake."

He was right, Debbie realized, and even if she wouldn't have described the cake in those terms, the structures were the same. If she used a larger dowel in the center, could she attach the layers to create the same cascade effect as Caroline's original cake? "I could always add extra support beneath each of the layers, too. Ones that would go down to the base at the bottom. You'd be able to see it from the back of the cake, but not from the front."

"And you could always scale this down a little, too. This thing has—what? Seven layers? You could cut back to five and still have the same look overall."

"No, I think I could still do all seven. Because, look, if I had the layers overlap a little more, I could still use regular dowels hidden inside the cake to support the tier above. And I—I can do this, Drew."

"I never had a doubt."

"But—what about tonight? I'd have to start baking right away to give the cakes time to chill before I can decorate and stack them."

"There will be other nights. I promise you that. But

right now, it's time for you to play heroine, to ride to the rescue and save Caroline's wedding day."

Fueled by half a pot of coffee and the challenge of recreating the original wedding cake, Debbie was up at four in the morning leveling the first and largest layer of the cake. She'd baked the seven layers of chocolate cake the night before after checking with Andrea to make sure the family had no chocolate allergies to worry about. The cakes had chilled in the refrigerator while she'd grabbed a few hours' sleep, making them slightly less fragile and easier to work with.

A soft knock at the back door took her by surprise. She wasn't expecting Kayla for another hour, but it wasn't her assistant who greeted her with a smile.

"Vanessa! What are you doing here?"

"My son has called me in for reinforcement. He says you have a wedding cake to make and no time to do your usual baking, so he asked me to lend a hand." The older woman's eyes sparkled, and Debbie didn't even want to guess what Drew's mother was thinking about her son's request. "I'll be the first to admit, I've never been paid for any of the meals I've made over the years—unless you count the praise and gratitude of my hungry family—but I can say with all honesty that I am an amazing cook."

"Of course you are!" Debbie readily agreed, but she never would have thought to ask for help. "Part of me can't believe Drew did this, but the other part knows I shouldn't have expected anything less."

"He is a rather remarkable boy, if I do say so myself."

Debbie might have argued the "boy" part, but as for the rest— "I couldn't agree more."

"Now, Kayla and I are going to do the baking and run the front of the shop and finish all the prep work for tomorrow. You focus on making a dream wedding cake for that poor couple, and we will do our best just to stay out of the way."

Debbie wasn't sure what it would be like to have another cook in the kitchen, but she was too grateful to Vanessa and to Drew for thinking about her to do anything but agree. She shouldn't have worried. Kayla and Vanessa worked together as seamlessly as if they'd done so for years, leaving Debbie to focus solely on the wedding cake. She crumb coated the cakes with buttercream icing, adding a layer of Bavarian cream between, and covered each one with fondant. She used a diamond-shaped cutter to press the quilt pattern into the thick frosting. She built one tier on top of the other until all seven formed the perfect spiral. She replaced the strawberry flowers with ones made of fondant in the same pinkish-red color.

By the time she was done, her back and shoulders ached, but being tired and sore wasn't enough to keep her from smiling at the cake—a darn close replica to Caroline's original choice if she did say so herself, minus the offending fruit.

"Oh, Debbie. It's just beautiful," Vanessa said, her proud smile once again reminding Debbie of her own mother.

"I just hope Caroline likes it."

"How could she not?"

Andrea had arranged for the caterers to pick up the cake in their van, and Debbie followed them to Hillcrest House, the site of the wedding and reception. The ballroom's darkly paneled walls and rich furnishings made for a perfect backdrop for the white cake. She made a few touch-ups once the cake was moved to the serving table and then stepped back to let Caroline and Andrea see the last-minute replacement.

"It's perfect. Just…perfect. I don't know how you did

it, but it's amazing. Thank you!" Caroline gushed. The blond bride looked gorgeous in a sheath-style gown with her hair caught up in a simple twist. Tears filled her eyes as she gazed at the cake, and Andrea quickly started to hustle her away before she could ruin her makeup.

"You are a lifesaver," the older woman vowed. "My future grandchildren thank you."

"Mom! Seriously?"

Debbie laughed at the exasperation in Caroline's voice even as she took another moment to look at the cake. She'd done it. Made a beautiful cake in a short period of time, but more than that, she'd silenced her own doubts. *This* was what she wanted to do. The creativity and challenge of making wedding cakes would never get old. Neither would seeing the joy in a bride's eyes when she saw her cake for the first time.

It was late by the time Debbie returned to the bakery, past closing time, so she was surprised to see the lights still on in the back. She hoped Vanessa and Kayla hadn't thought they needed to stick around until she returned. The two of them had already gone beyond the call of duty to have taken over for her the way they had.

But when she opened the door, it wasn't the two women who were waiting for her. Instead Drew sat at the butcher-block island with a couple of disposable take-out containers in front of him. "Drew, what are you doing here?"

"My mom told me that you worked all day with no more than a few minutes' break. I figured you were probably starving but wouldn't bother to eat if you had to make dinner for yourself."

"You're right." Debbie dropped onto the stool he pulled over for her and closed her eyes. The scent of barbecue teased her senses and made her mouth water, but she was so tired she didn't know if she could stay awake long enough to eat.

"Hey, come on, Sleeping Beauty. You've got to eat something. Brides are going to be beating your door down when word gets out about that cake you made, so you've got to keep your strength up."

Smiling, Debbie opened her eyes. "You should have seen the cake, Drew."

He laughed. "Do you really think my mom didn't take a ton of pictures and send them to me? She was so thrilled to help out today."

"Thank you for that. She was a lifesaver. I don't know what I would have done without her."

And she didn't know what she would have done without Drew. He'd encouraged her to go after her dreams, to believe they could still come true. And if she wasn't so exhausted, she would have loved to show him just how grateful she was.

But she barely managed to eat half of the barbecue sandwich he'd picked up for her before her eyes started to close. After packing up the leftovers and stashing them in the refrigerator, Drew pulled Debbie up from the stool. He wrapped an arm around her shoulders as he led her up the stairs to her bedroom.

Gazing with longing at her bed, Debbie sighed. She was torn between sleeping…and sleeping with Drew. A giant yawn came out of nowhere, seeming to give her the answer she needed. "I'm sorry, Drew. I'm just—exhausted."

"I know. Which is why I'm putting you to bed and not taking you to bed."

True to his word, Drew guided her to the bathroom and waited while she stumbled through changing into her pajamas, washing her face and brushing her teeth. He had the covers on her bed turned back for her, and Debbie had to smile as she remembered the night at his house when he'd sent her off to bed with nothing more than a kiss on the forehead.

Exhausted or not, she wasn't letting him get away with it a second time. Slipping between the sheets, she held out a hand to him. "Stay with me?"

Drew froze for a split second before taking her hand. "Are you sure?"

She smiled sleepily. "Stay."

Two nights with too little sleep should have left Debbie feeling exhausted, but she couldn't keep the smile off her face or a softly hummed tune from her lips as she opened the bakery the next morning. She wasn't sure what time it had been when she and Drew had awoken and reached for each other, but the inky darkness only added to the intimacy as they explored each other using other senses—touch, taste, sound. And she hadn't needed to see the satisfied smile on Drew's face to know she'd put it there.

She couldn't recall a time when she'd been so happy, and if at times a worried whisper slipped through her thoughts, questioning how long such happiness could last, Debbie brushed it away.

The bell above the door rang, and Debbie looked up to see Evelyn McClaren step inside. The fiftysomething woman owned and ran Hillcrest House, and she glanced at the Halloween decorations scattered throughout the bakery as if wondering if she'd entered the right shop.

Debbie had only met the other woman a few times, and she was as stylish and businesslike as ever in her straight red skirt and matching jacket. Her auburn hair was caught up in a twist; her makeup and jewelry were understated and impeccable. She was also extremely thin and fit, looking at least a decade younger than her age, and not someone who normally—if ever—visited the bakery. "Mrs. McClaren, good morning. What can I get for you?"

A small smile curved the woman's lips as if she'd guessed Debbie's thoughts. "I'll have a cup of coffee, please."

Curious about the reason for the businesswoman's visit, she lifted the pot of freshly brewed dark roast and poured a cup. After accepting the steaming mug, Evelyn got right down to business. "I have a proposition for you, Ms. Mattson," she said, eyeing her over the rim once she'd taken a sip. "Hillcrest House has a reputation locally as the place to go for special occasions—engagement parties, weddings, anniversaries. But it's always been my goal to reach outside of our little town." The slightest hint of sarcasm touched the woman's last words, giving away the fact that Evelyn McClaren clearly still thought of the big city as her home—despite living in little Clearville.

"Now more and more of the couples who come to Hillcrest to get married are from out of town. And as many opportunities as that presents, it also can present problems—like what happened last weekend with Caroline Collins's wedding."

"But Caroline's from Clearville," Debbie pointed out.

"True. But the bakery she chose was up in Portland, and the flowers came from Sacramento and the band she hired was from San Francisco—" Evelyn waived a dismissive hand. "Getting married might be a wonderful, romantic event for the bride and groom, but for me, it's business. And in business, the closer the relationship you have with those you work with, the better off you will be. Which is why I'm interested in offering all-inclusive wedding packages for tourists and locals alike. The resort will handle everything—from the music, to the photographer, to the flowers and the cake. And that is where you come in."

"Me?" Debbie kept her jaw from dropping, but just barely.

"Andrea Collins thinks you are a lifesaver, and I agree. Her daughter was a tissue or two away from calling off the whole wedding, and the inn's cancellation policy wouldn't have come close to covering the losses at such a late date. The cake you made was gorgeous—and delicious, from the comments I overheard. I would expect that from any baker, but the way you worked under pressure and stepped up to help simply because someone asked, that's what truly impressed me."

"I— Thank you. I was happy to help." And Drew was right—it had felt good to ride in and save the day. She'd never imagined it would lead to this kind of offer from the biggest resort in town. A buzz vibrated beneath her skin, and she could barely hold still. And the more she and the other woman talked, the stronger that feeling grew until she felt ready to bounce off the ceiling like a kid on a sugar high from too many of her Halloween cookies.

"I'll want your input regarding the different flavors and fillings to offer in the packages, and I'll need photographs of the designs that will be available. Of course, the size of the cake and number of layers will depend on the number of guests. Once the holiday rush is over, we'll be ready to focus on spring weddings, so I'll want everything finalized in the next few weeks. I assume that won't be a problem."

"I could have some tasting cakes ready by this weekend. If you have any of the menus set for the reception dinners, I could see if there's a certain flavor of cake that would complement the entrees."

"I'll send you what our chef has come up with so far." They spoke for a few more minutes before Evelyn said, "I think this partnership will benefit us both, and of course, all the credit for the wedding cakes will go to you and your bakery."

Debbie accepted the businesswoman's card but waved aside her offer to pay for the coffee. Promising to be in touch, Evelyn turned and walked out on her three-inch heels. With echo of the bell still ringing in her ears, Debbie held tight to the small card—proof that the past few minutes hadn't been an illusion. Evelyn wouldn't be an easy woman to work for, but the opportunity was still too incredible to possibly pass up.

It was exactly what she wanted—a chance to find her own success in the bakery that still bore her mother's name. After so many years of keeping her mother's dream alive, this was her one shot to live her own, and she couldn't let anything stand in her way. The partnership with the inn would mean a lot of hard work and sacrifice, but that at least was nothing new.

After all, the bakery had always come first.

Drew wasn't sure what to expect when Debbie asked him to come over that evening. She'd told him she had some exciting news to share, but something in her voice was off. Something that sounded more nervous than excited.

When he walked into the bakery, he could see she'd been baking up a storm. The sink was filled with mixing bowls and cake pans and a dozen or so cakes lined the cooling racks. She was whipping something in a stainless-steel bowl, the whisk moving so fast it became little more than a metallic blur in her hand.

"Give me just a second. This whipped cream is almost ready."

"You've been busy. Is this another round of taste tests for the new menu?"

"Not exactly." Seeming satisfied with the peaks in the cream, she set the bowl aside to face him. She took a deep breath, and a bad feeling settled in Drew's gut. Whatever news she had to share, he already knew he wasn't going to like hearing it.

"Evelyn McClaren stopped by today."

As she filled him in on the conversation she'd had with the inn owner, Drew thought maybe he'd misread the situation. Maybe it was just Debbie's nerves he was picking up on and he'd imagined the rest.

"That's great, Debbie! I'm so proud of you." But when he stepped closer, he knew it wasn't his imagination that she took a small step back. The movement was slight. Just the tiniest step, but Drew swallowed, seeing it for the chasm it truly was.

"The thing is, I'm going to be really busy the next few weeks coming up with the perfect cakes and decorations, and then I have Kara and Sam's wedding cake to bake on top of all that. If this partnership with Hillcrest House takes off the way I hope it will, I'll have to hire on more help. But that won't be for several months."

"What are you saying, Debbie?"

"I just think it might be time for us to take a step back."

A step back? Most days he felt like he barely had a toe-hold into her life as it was. "Back to what, exactly?"

She hesitated. "Just being friends."

He couldn't believe it. "Because you've let me so far in already."

Her chin rose at his burst of sarcasm, her expression so stubborn and so beautiful it hurt him to look at her. "We agreed. This was just supposed to be a fling."

Drew swore beneath his breath. "Don't give me that! It's been more than a fling from the start, and you know it."

Crossing her arms over her apron, she said, "I told you I wasn't looking for anything serious. You agreed."

"I don't agree with you kicking me to the curb because you're scared to realize how serious our relationship already is."

"I am not scared! This is my chance to go after my dream, and I'm taking it! This time I'm not going to let anything stand in my way."

The blow she landed hit him square in the chest, knocking more than just the wind out of him. Somehow it shattered what was left of his hope. "Is that what you think I do? Stand in the way of your happiness?"

"No, not— No. But I need to focus and not leave myself open to…distractions."

"Distractions. Right." Because that was what she was reducing their relationship to. The distraction of a meaningless fling.

Hurt and frustration boiled up inside him, and the hell of it was Drew couldn't even say that she hadn't warned him. Debbie had always said the bakery came first. But he'd never expected to find himself so completely out of the running.

Chapter Twelve

"What's this I hear about you not staying open for Halloween night?" Sophia demanded as she walked through the bakery's back door and into the kitchen.

"Who told you—" Debbie didn't need to finish the question as Kayla guiltily ducked her head and muttered something about making sure everything was locked up out front.

Planting her hands on her hips, her friend looked just like she had when they'd argued as kids. Well, except for her expanding belly. But the stubborn lift to her jaw and flashing eyes were still the same. "You always stay open late on Halloween for the kids to trick-or-treat here before they head over to the Fall Fest in the town square!"

"I've just been too busy this year to even think about it. The other stores on Main Street will still be open— including The Hope Chest—so it's not like the kids will be disappointed."

"It's not the kids I'm worried about. You love dressing up every year almost as much as you love seeing the kids in their costumes and passing out miniature cookies for them to eat!"

She *did* love dressing up. So much so that she'd bought a costume a few weeks ago. An ice-blue ball gown complete with white, elbow-length gloves, a sparkling tiara and glass—well, clear plastic—slippers. Her hand lifted to a real glass slipper—the tiny crystal pendant Drew had given her—and the one she hadn't been able to take off.

"I just—can't." To her horror, her eyes filled with tears, and she couldn't look away fast enough to hide them from Sophia.

Sympathy softened her friend's expression for a split second before her typical drill-sergeant personality took over. Grabbing Debbie's arm, she practically dragged her from the kitchen to the stair that led to the apartment above.

"The bakery—"

"Kayla will finish up anything that needs to be done. That's why you hired her." Marching her over to the living room's small, shabby-chic love seat, Sophia settled Debbie against the cushions before raiding her bathroom for a box of tissue and her kitchen for a pint of mint-chocolate-chip ice cream and two spoons. "Now tell me," she said with a sigh, "how badly do I have to beat up Drew?"

Almost choking on her first frozen bite, Debbie stared at her friend. "You—knew?"

"Of course I knew! You're my best friend and Drew's my brother. Did you really think I wouldn't notice something going on between the two of you?"

"You never said anything..."

"Because you weren't talking! But I did warn Drew

that I'd hurt him if he hurt you. So tell me, how badly do I need to beat him up?"

Her eyes burning with tears again, Debbie stuck the spoon back into the ice cream, unable to eat another bite.

"That bad, huh?"

"No, and that's what makes it so sad." Pressing the heels of her hands against her eyes, she admitted, "It wasn't Drew. It was me."

"Well, I guess I should be glad about that, at least. Don't tell Nick or Sam, but Drew's always been my favorite brother." That got a short laugh out of Debbie as Sophia pulled her hands from her face and passed her several tissues. "So I guess my next question is how badly did you hurt *him?*"

"Oh, Sophia. I never meant to." And just like that, the whole story came pouring out—from the moment Drew had overheard them at the bachelorette party to when he'd walked out a few days before.

"He was right, too. I am scared. I don't know how to handle this opportunity with Hillcrest House and still make time for a relationship. If I blow this chance with Evelyn, what if I end up blaming and resenting Drew? And if I focus too much on the bakery, then he'll just end up resenting me."

She took a deep breath and looked over to her best friend for comfort and support and—

Sophia lifted a shoulder in a casual shrug. "Other couples juggle jobs and relationships all the time."

"What?"

"Well, they do. Jake and I manage even with all the work he does out of town. Nick and Darcy. Sam and Kara. We've all made it work."

"Okay, well, thank you very much for the pep talk that's made me feel like an even bigger failure."

"You're not a failure, but I don't think you're being totally honest with yourself about what it is you're truly afraid of."

"This partnership with Hillcrest House is a really big deal. What else would I be afraid of?"

After setting the ice cream on the beat-up steamer trunk Debbie used for a coffee table, Sophia picked up the framed photograph sitting there. The last picture taken of her father before he died. "He's the only other man you've ever loved, and you lost him," Sophia said softly.

Tracing a finger over the cool, smooth glass, Debbie argued, "I was just a kid. I don't even remember…"

Except that wasn't true. Not entirely. A memory, far more faded and faint than the picture in the frame, lingered in her mind. Her birthday party the year she turned four. She'd invited friends from preschool and had worn a new dress. The cake her mother made had been enormous in her childish mind—bigger than she was—with layer after pink layer reaching to the ceiling.

Her father hadn't been there, but a calendar had hung on the refrigerator, and each day she and her mother had marked off another day. First counting down to her birthday and then to the day when her daddy would be home. And she'd been so excited… She'd closed her eyes tight when she'd blown out those candles, wishing so hard that when she opened them, her daddy would already be there—

Opening her eyes over twenty-two years later, he still wasn't there.

Maybe it was that moment when she was a little girl—or maybe it was years later when her mother was diagnosed with cancer—that she'd stopped wishing, stopped hoping, stopped believing. And in place of wishes and hope and faith, fear had taken root. The fear that nothing good could last and that *temporary* was all she could count on.

She'd been right about Drew all along. He wasn't a temporary kind of guy. He was the kind of man a woman could love forever—if she was brave enough to trust in a forever love.

"You're right. I'm afraid of how much I already love Drew. I did my best to minimize what we had and to keep him at a distance and it still didn't work. I still fell in love with him, and if I lost him—the way my mom lost my dad—"

"Sweetie, you know how much your mom loved your dad and how much she missed him, but don't you think if she had the chance to do it all over again, she would? In a heartbeat? Because that's what love is. It's a celebration of the time we do have together—whether that's decades or even only days."

"She would have lost him a hundred times as long as it meant she had the chance to love him first." Wiping at her eyes, she looked at her friend. "So what do I do? How do I fix things with Drew?"

"Well, first off, you're staying open late for Halloween and you're coming to the Fall Fest."

"Seriously?" Debbie fell back against the cushions with a faint laugh.

"Yes, I take all holidays very seriously. Now tell me— because I know you already have one—what's your costume for this year?"

Heaving a sigh, she admitted, "Cinderella."

Sophia's clapped her hands together. "Yes! That is just perfect."

"Why?"

"Because," she said with a matchmaking twinkle in her dark eyes, "I am your fairy godmother."

* * *

True to her word, Sophia arrived the afternoon of Halloween to help with the magical transformation of turning Debbie into a princess. She had to admit her friend had done an amazing job with her makeup and hair, sweeping her blond curls into a cartoon-perfect twist.

The only change Debbie made to the costume was passing up the glass slippers for the heels Drew had bought for her. Not that anyone could see them beneath the gown's full skirt, but she felt a little more hopeful simply knowing she was wearing them.

And she could use all the hope and all the help she could get.

No matter how many times she asked Sophia, her friend had refused to tell Debbie how she planned to get Drew to come to the Fall Fest that night.

"Trust me," Sophia promised when she stopped by the bakery looking adorable in green leggings and an orange sweatshirt with a grinning black jack-o'-lantern face over her pregnant belly.

"Drew will be there. Just make sure you get to the square before midnight," she teased with a wink.

"I'm closing up at seven. I think I'll make it," she said as she handed out another bite-size cookie, this time to a toddler dressed in the cutest black-and-red ladybug outfit. She couldn't help smiling as the delicate little girl tried to shove her whole fist, cookie and all, into her mouth, much to her mother's embarrassment.

The festival was in full swing by the time Debbie arrived. The cool evening air was filled with the scents of fried food, kettle corn and the hay bales scattered around for seating and ambiance. The town square was decorated in the orange and black of Halloween along with the rich, vibrant colors of fall. Music drifted above the sounds of talking and laughter, and she saw that the local cover band had taken its place on the stage.

Looking around for her friends, she spotted Sam Pirelli first. Dressed in full Captain Jack Sparrow regalia, complete with hat, eyeliner and dreadlocks, he was hard to miss. Kara stood alongside him, looking at once embarrassed and yet proud to have such a good-looking, if outrageous, fiancé. Jake Cameron, Sophia's husband, hadn't dressed up, but he stood behind his wife, his arms wrapped around their "pumpkin" in the oven.

Debbie knew Kara hadn't wanted Timmy out too late and figured his grandparents had already taken him home. Nick's daughter, Maddie, had stopped by the bakery earlier with a group of friends, giving Nick and Darcy a night alone.

Which left only one Pirelli unaccounted for.

As Debbie made her way through the crowd, the band switched to a ballad. First Sam and Kara, and then Sophia and Jake stepped onto the makeshift dance floor. Debbie's footsteps slowed as the couples wrapped their arms around each other and gazed into one another's eyes. As much as she loved spending time with her friends, did she really want to play the part of the fifth wheel throughout the evening if Drew didn't show?

She pulled the white shawl she'd added to help ward off the October chill a little closer. Her pale blue skirt rustled against her legs, and while she certainly wasn't the only one in costume, she was starting to feel all dressed up with no place to go.

Drew had done some foolish things in his life. A man could hardly reach the age of thirty without having more than a few what-the-hell-was-I-thinking moments, but he was pretty sure tonight might end up taking the cake.

Walking toward the square, he stopped short as he caught sight of himself in a darkened store window. In a small town like Clearville, businesses shut down in the early evening on most nights. They certainly did on nights when the town had an event like the Fall Fest planned.

The event would run for hours, starting with little kids trick-or-treating throughout town rather than trying to go from house to house where neighbors were separated by several acres of land. After that, families would head toward the town square. Costume contests and pie throwing and pumpkin carving were all scheduled, and he could already hear music from a local band playing. A cheer rose as they switched to a classic-rock song with a pulsing beat guaranteed to get the crowd jumping and bounce the slow dancers off the floor.

But it was still early. Early enough for him to go home and change.

The wavy image in the storefront window seemed to urge him to do just that. To change his clothes and change his mind and maybe not make a total ass out of himself.

Why had he listened to Sophia in the first place? For all he knew this was some kind of setup, payback for him pulling her pigtails one too many times back when they were kids. Except his sister wasn't the type to kick a man when he was down, and there was no question that was how she'd found him when she'd stopped by his house the day before.

He'd crashed on the couch, Rain by his side, as he'd tried to watch the midweek football game. By the third quarter, the contest was a rout, but that had little to do with his lack of attention.

Had he really read Debbie so wrong? He'd been so sure she wanted more than casual, more than temporary. Had he only seen what he wanted to see?

He heard the knock on his front door a split second before the sound of it opening, signaling it was a member of his nosy family. Rain jumped down to welcome the visitor, and his sister greeted the dog in a high-pitched voice guaranteed to set the puppy shaking with excitement.

"The point of knocking," he told her as she carried the ecstatic puppy back into the living room, "is to wait for the person inside to let you in."

Dropping onto the couch beside him, she lifted her chin out of the way of Rain's darting tongue. "Thought I'd save you the trouble."

After circling a few times, the puppy settled into what was left of Sophia's lap, both of them looking like they planned to stay there awhile. "What do you want, Soph?"

"To tell you that I talked to Debbie."

"Well, then, you know you don't have to worry about me breaking her heart anymore, do you?"

"You know she loves you, right?"

Drew could stand to hear a lot of things, but that wasn't one of them. Pushing off the couch, he glared down at his little sister. "Give me a break. You were there the night of Darcy's bachelorette party. You heard what Debbie wanted. Some guy to have a fling with. And that's all it was."

That was all *he* was.

"You don't really believe that."

"She made it pretty clear."

"She's afraid of how she really feels. So maybe she was looking for an easy out, and what did you do but take it?"

Drew tossed up his hands in exasperation. "How did this end up being my fault?"

Sophia struggled to get to her feet but couldn't quite manage thanks to the low-slung couch and the puppy in her lap. She set the puppy back on the floor and pushed up from the cushions. "Because, Drew, when the woman you love walks away, you don't let her go. You go after her!"

Maybe it spoke to his desperation that he'd been so quick to listen to Sophia, to believe he and Debbie still had a chance. Why else would he have agreed to show up to the festival in costume? He never dressed up, leaving that to Sam, who always went all out without the slightest bit of embarrassment. Drew felt as self-conscious as hell, but he'd promised he would attend the event and that he would try to convince Debbie to give their relationship another try. An *honest* try.

Making his decision, he continued walking toward the square. As the sounds of the music and scents of fried foods grew stronger, he slipped through the crowd gathered near the food booths.

"Well, if it isn't Prince Charming!"

Drew's face heated and his temper started to burn at the hoot of laughter as he turned to face his younger brother. Or at least he thought it was Sam. It was a little hard to tell under the eyeliner and black dreads. "That's the guy from Snow White. I'm supposed to be the one from Cinderella."

"Oh, well, yeah. 'Cause that makes it so much less lame."

"Shut up, Captain Jack."

Drew took a deep breath, reminding himself what was at stake and why he'd been willing to put on the blue uniform with its bright gold buttons, red sash and epaulets. Gold-freakin'-tasseled epaulets.

"Why don't both of you chill. This is a party, remember? And I'm ready for a good time." Ryder Kincaid was wearing his football jersey from high school and had his Wildcat helmet tucked beneath his arm. Exchanging a look with Sam, he asked, "So you really think I should I ask her out?"

"Oh, yeah! Why not, right? She's pretty, sexy, funny— available."

Still searching the crowd, Drew barely paid attention to the conversation between the other two men until one word jumped out at him and he froze. Turning back, he demanded, "What did you say about Debbie?"

Ryder grinned. "That she's turned out to be pretty hot. I mean, I don't really remember her that well from high school, but when your sister set us up the other night, I thought I hit the jackpot. I figure it's time for me to dive back into the dating pool."

Grinding his back teeth together, Drew gritted out, "Find another girl."

"Why? I mean, we're both single. Or at least she is, and I will be as soon as the divorce goes through, so—"

Drew didn't stop to think. Stepping closer, he repeated, "Find another girl, Kincaid."

"Wow, dude!" Sam threw an arm across Drew's chest and pulled him away from Ryder. Drew braced himself, waiting for the other man to retaliate, but the tension slowly eased from his body as he realized Ryder wasn't angry. Instead he and Sam were grinning like a couple of idiots.

"I wouldn't have believed it if I hadn't seen it for myself," his brother said.

Holding out a hand, Ryder said, "Pay up, man."

Drew watched as Sam passed his newest employee twenty bucks, the last of his jealousy and anger dissolving into confusion. "What's going on?"

"Ryder told me you had a thing for Debbie, and I didn't believe it."

"I don't have a thing for her."

"Yeah, what would you call it?"

"I don't know, Sam. How do you describe the way you feel about Kara?" Drew shot back.

His younger brother sobered almost instantly. "It's that serious?"

Drew sighed. "It is for me."

"Then why are you standing around with the two of us?" Ryder asked.

"Ryder's right. Go get her, Cinderella Man!"

"Sam, I swear..." Drew was shaking his head as he walked away. But he was smiling, too.

Debbie did eventually join her girlfriends on the edge of the dance floor. She was doing her best to try to have a good time, but her heart wasn't in it. She wondered how long she would have to stay before she could slip away and head home.

"Don't worry. He'll be here," Sophia promised.

"How can you be so sure? Maybe he changed his mind. Maybe he doesn't think I'm worth it after the way I pushed him away."

"I'm sure." Her friend's smile grew wider. "Fairy tales always end happily ever after."

"My life has never been much of a fairy tale, Sophia."

"It is tonight," Sophia whispered as she placed her hands on Debbie's shoulders and tuned her toward the dance floor.

Debbie gasped as she caught sight of Drew cutting his way through the crowd. He was here. Making his way toward her. The sights and sounds of the festival faded away. The distance between them lessened until she could feel the heat of his gaze wash over her.

A trembling smile crossed her face as the crowd finally parted, and she caught sight of what he was wearing. The classic prince costume—the royal blue coat, the gold buttons, the red sash. He looked incredible, if completely uncomfortable, which only made her love him that much more.

He moved toward her without breaking stride, not stopping until he stood a few feet in front of her and held out his hand. Placing her gloved hand in his, she followed him onto the dance floor. The band started to play, and she couldn't help but give a small laugh as she recognized the first few notes of the classic Celine Dion soundtrack.

"I know tonight is all about fantasy and make-believe," he told her, "but what I want is real. A real relationship. One that's out in the open, for all our friends and family to see. One that's important enough to come first in both of our lives."

"Drew, I'm so sorry for everything I said. For pushing you away. I don't want to hide how I feel anymore."

Grinning, he said, "Well, that's a good thing considering the cat's pretty much out of the bag now."

She laughed, tears shimmering in her eyes, and then a playful grin lit up her face. "Well, considering half the town seems to be watching, I think we might as well give them something to see, don't you?"

Pulling his head down, Debbie pressed her mouth to his, relishing the freedom to kiss him and not care who was watching. A few catcalls came from the crowd, and she felt his smile before he backed away. "Let's not give them too much to see."

Drew wasn't sure when he became aware of a sound beyond the crowd of people around them, beyond the music from the stage. The sound of shouting and the faint wail of sirens growing louder. Closer.

He saw people around him exchanging worried looks as a ripple moved through the crowd. He caught only a couple of words, but they were enough to send a shiver of concern racing through him.

Smoke...Main Street...fire department...
And a word he hoped Debbie hadn't heard.
Grabbing his arm, color faded from her face as she whispered, "The bakery."

Chapter Thirteen

In the harsh light of morning, the destruction of the bakery was even more apparent than it had been the night before. The plate-glass window had been broken out, the shelves and register inside nothing more than charred ruins. She didn't know the extent of the damage to the kitchen or her apartment upstairs. The fire department had yet to declare the structure safe to enter.

"Are you sure you want to be here, Debbie?" Sophia asked gently.

Jake and Sophia had brought her home with them the night before. Drew had wanted to take her back to his place, but even in her dazed state, she'd heard Sophia's whispered reminder that Debbie wouldn't have anything else to wear. Her whole wardrobe was now limited to a Halloween costume.

Tonight is about fantasy.

Drew's words echoed in her head, and she fought the

crazy urge to laugh. Well, today was just chock full of reality, wasn't it?

"This isn't a good idea," Drew muttered. "Come on, Debbie. Let's go."

Sympathy filled his dark eyes, and she had to look away. She couldn't face it, couldn't face him, with the ugly, destructive mass of guilt building up inside her. How many times had she felt like she was trapped by the business her mother had loved, by the legacy Bonnie had left behind? How many times, in the darkest places of her heart, had she secretly resented it? She couldn't believe that bitter acid of resentment had eaten away at the ancient wiring, but that didn't mean this wasn't some kind of a sign.

She'd wanted her freedom, and now she had it. She'd felt shackled to the business, and now that it was in ruins, those chains slipped way.

"It's all my fault."

"Don't!" Grabbing her shoulders, he turned her away from the building. "Don't say that. We don't even know what caused the fire."

"You warned me about the wiring, and I didn't listen."

He swore under his breath. "Even if it was the wiring, I didn't honestly suspect there was a problem. If I had, don't you think I would have insisted on checking it out myself? And doesn't that make this more my fault than yours?"

His grip eased as he slid his hands down her arms. He linked his fingers with hers, but Debbie was too numb to feel it. "We're going to fix this, Debbie. It'll only take a few weeks, and everything will be back to the way it was."

Debbie gave a rough laugh. The way it was. The way it would always be if she didn't take the chance fate had handed her. "Maybe I don't want to fix it."

"What are you talking about? You can't just leave it—"

"Why not? Those 'few weeks' will make it too late for

me to take the partnership with Hillcrest that Evelyn offered. You can't fix that, Drew, any more than you can fix the bakery. Bonnie's Bakery is gone. I wanted freedom and now—" She waved a hand at the smoke-scarred, water-stained building. "There's nothing left for me here."

Drew flinched as if she'd struck him. "Nothing?" he echoed flatly. "What about us, Debbie? Or is that nothing, too? I love you. Can you really still not see that? I'm in love with you."

Pain clutched her throat, each word jagged and cutting as she tried to get them out. "I don't— I can't—"

Sophia wrapped an arm around her shoulders and led Debbie away. "Come on. Let's go."

Jake clamped a hand on Drew's shoulder and quietly advised, "She's still in shock. Give her time."

Drew nodded, but he knew all the time in the world wouldn't matter if Debbie didn't love him back.

"You do realize that one of these days you're going to have to leave this room," Sophia said as she walked into the guest bedroom where Debbie had been staying since the fire. A guest bedroom Sophia was gradually turning into a nursery.

Along with the small twin bed where Debbie had holed up, a white crib, matching dresser and a bookshelf filled the room. Sophia's baby already had an accumulation of toys lining the shelves, with more to come once Sophia had her shower in a few weeks.

"I figure I'll wait until your little guy or girl comes along."

"That's not for another two months."

Debbie nodded as she tucked a stray curl behind her ear. She knew it was only her imagination because she'd thoroughly washed her hair since the fire, but the stench of smoke still seemed to cling to everything she touched. Even food tasted like ash. "Two months sounds about right."

"Deb..." Sophia sank onto the bed beside her, pulling away the cream-colored ruffled pillow she had been holding to her chest like some kind of shield.

"I just—can't. It's like the days after my mom died all over again. With everyone being so sympathetic and so nice, and I just don't have the strength to pretend everything's fine."

"Good grief, Debbie! Everything is not fine, and no one expects you to pretend that it is! You've lost your business and your home, and people want to help. That's what we do around here. You know that."

"Everything's—gone. There's nothing anyone can do about that."

"You're so sure about that?"

Unable to hold Sophia's steady gaze, Debbie glanced down at the sea-green comforter. She knew her friend had overheard Drew's heartfelt declaration and her own cold, empty silence.

Huffing a sigh, Sophia reached into the pocket of her flowery maternity dress. "Well, at least listen to your messages. Your phone hasn't stopped ringing in the past two days."

Her phone. She'd forgotten that it, too, hadn't been lost in the fire, having thrown it into her small evening bag on Halloween night at the last minute. Swiping the screen, she blinked, startled to realize Sophia hadn't exaggerated about the number of calls.

The first was from Kayla, and Debbie cringed. She should have been the one to call her employee. In the background, she could hear Kayla's baby girl's sweet babbling, but the young woman didn't say anything about her job or ask when she might be able to come back to work. She simply said how sorry she was and asked Debbie to call if she needed anything.

The next message was from Vanessa Pirelli, who volunteered to help at the bakery again anytime Debbie might need her. Andrea Collins reminded Debbie that she worked in real estate and could help her find a temporary rental space until the bakery was up and running again. Hope Daniels offered her a place to stay in the apartment above the antiques store.

And another message was from Evelyn McClaren, who offered her the use of Hillcrest's kitchen for her baking, not wanting Debbie to fall behind on wedding cake selections they still needed to finalize for the inn's all-inclusive wedding packages.

Other messages were from friends and acquaintances—all telling her they couldn't wait for the bakery to open again and offering their help just as Sophia had said.

How had she missed that? How had she become so focused on what muffins she made or what cupcakes she sold that she stopped thinking about the customers and friends she saw—sometimes every day. And had she really believed that the *bakery* was the only thing tying her to Clearville?

She couldn't leave this town she loved any more than she could leave the man she loved. But of all the messages she'd played back on her phone, not one of them had been from Drew.

He told you he loved you, and you just walked away.

He'd already come back to her once after she'd pushed him away. Did she really think he'd chase after her again?

It was definitely her turn.

Drew stared at the under-construction house and wondered if he'd ever be able to finish it. What would be the point when the family he'd built it for—the family of his dreams—seemed more out of reach than ever? He couldn't stand the thought of living there alone. And yet the idea of another family moving in made him want to tear the place down with his bare hands. Board by board, nail by nail, until there was nothing left.

When he'd been a kid, he'd broken a rib once while roughhousing with Nick. He still remembered the stabbing pain with every breath he took. That pain was back. Only now it was his raw and bruised heart aching on each and every breath, and no tightly wrapped bandage was going to take that hurt away.

This was different from the first time, though he still couldn't believe he was fool enough to have let Debbie trample his heart *twice*. The night in the bakery, they'd argued. They'd both lost their temper, hurling accusations and saying things they didn't mean. Deep down, though, he'd still had hope that he could fix things.

You can't fix this.

Debbie's broken, aching words added a dull throb to the already stabbing pain, and he hunched his shoulders beneath the leather jacket he wore. She was right, of course. His offer had been stupid and meaningless. The bakery was more than a building. More than new floors and walls and windows. She'd told him once that keeping the bakery the same as it was when her mother was alive was a way for her to keep Bonnie's memory alive.

Did he really think he could recreate those memories by slapping up a new coat of bright and shiny pink paint?

He kicked his work boot at the loose rocks along the driveway. That was as stupid as thinking if he built this house that the family he'd always imagined would come.

He should turn Ryder loose on the place. Let the other man finish it and put the house up for sale.

There's nothing left for me here.

Yeah, he was starting to know the feeling.

The crunch of gravel alerted him to a car's approach, and he hoped it wasn't Sophia or another member of his family—but the familiar lime-green Bug didn't belong to Sophia. And his stupid heart started pounding against his chest, ready and willing to throw itself out there to get trampled a third time.

He soaked in the sight of her, as if it had been two years instead of the two days since he'd last seen her. She looked tired. Her hair was caught back in a low ponytail, her face washed clean of makeup and she was wearing his sister's borrowed clothes. And he'd never seen her look more beautiful. Because despite all those things, when she met his gaze she lifted her chin, holding her head high. Still strong, still a fighter, still the girl he'd fallen in love with—hell, maybe as far back as the day of her mother's funeral.

"I was wrong." Her voice carried across the cool, crisp morning air, her misty breath forming a cloud around her words. A bit of color came to her cheeks as she closed the space between them. "I want you to rebuild the bakery."

"So you're here looking for a contractor?"

She nodded. "A contractor, a white knight…the man I love."

Her voice caught on the last word, but it didn't matter. Drew still heard it. Still felt it shining in the bright blue of her eyes, in the warmth of her smile, and he realized he'd been wrong. As that feeling wrapped tight around his heart, all the pain *did* go away.

"God, Debbie, I am so sorry," he whispered as he pulled her into his arms. He breathed in the sweet smell of her shampoo as he held her tight. "About the fire. About acting like I could just ride to the rescue and make everything better."

"You can. You have."

"No, you were right. Offering to rebuild the bakery as if I could make it as good as new was stupid. I can't give you back all the memories you lost in the fire."

"Maybe not," she agreed as she pulled back just far enough to gaze up at him. Tears swam in her eyes, making the blue that much brighter, but he had no doubt that they were tears of joy, of hope. "But you can help me make new ones. I thought the fire was a chance to break free of the past, and maybe it is. But more than that, it's a chance for me to embrace the future. I want you to rebuild the bakery and to help me make it mine. The way you've built this house to be yours."

"This house isn't mine," he confessed with a shaky laugh. "It never was. It's always been ours. Whether I knew it or not, from the moment I broke ground, I was building it for us. For our family."

"I like the sound of that."

"Well, I hope you like the sound of this even more. I love you, Debbie Mattson. I love that you've been my friend all these years and that you know me so well and yet you never cease take me by surprise. I love that you were willing to give up your own dreams to take care of your mom and that you still have courage to go after them now."

"I'm glad you see me that way, but the truth is I've been a coward. I tried to tell myself that having a fling with you was my way of living in the moment, but instead it was just me hiding from my feelings. I think the best way to seize the day is to hold on to the people you love and never let them go."

"Where am I going to go when the woman I love is right here?"

"Well, you can't just stand around for too long. We have a future to build, remember?"

"That we do," he promised. "And you know, if you're going to rebuild the bakery of your dreams, you're going to need a new name."

"You're right. It's something I should have done a long time ago. Something my mother would have wanted me to do."

"Well, I've been thinking long and hard about this, and I've come up with the perfect choice."

Judging by the smile tugging at Debbie's lips, he wasn't doing a very good job keeping a straight face. "And what is that?"

"I was thinking…Pirelli's Pastries."

Debbie's laughter filled the morning air, and Drew didn't bother trying to hold back his smile as she threw her arms around his neck. "Is that a yes?"

"To marrying you? That's an absolute yes! To renaming the bakery? I think we need to give that one another try."

* * * * *

Theresa Pirelli had come to Clearville to escape her past—not look for love in all the wrong places! But when local cowboy Jarrett Deeks gets under her skin, the big-city nurse realizes she just might have the skill to heal both their wounded hearts....

Don't miss the next installment of Stacy Connelly's Special Edition miniseries
THE PIRELLI BROTHERS
Coming in early 2015!

REQUEST YOUR FREE BOOKS!
2 FREE NOVELS PLUS 2 FREE GIFTS!

Ⓗ HARLEQUIN®

SPECIAL EDITION

Life, Love & Family

YES! Please send me 2 FREE Harlequin® Special Edition novels and my 2 FREE gifts (gifts are worth about $10). After receiving them, if I don't wish to receive any more books, I can return the shipping statement marked "cancel." If I don't cancel, I will receive 6 brand-new novels every month and be billed just $4.74 per book in the U.S. or $5.24 per book in Canada. That's a savings of at least 14% off the cover price! It's quite a bargain! Shipping and handling is just 50¢ per book in the U.S. and 75¢ per book in Canada.* I understand that accepting the 2 free books and gifts places me under no obligation to buy anything. I can always return a shipment and cancel at any time. Even if I never buy another book, the two free books and gifts are mine to keep forever.

235/335 HDN F45Y

Name	(PLEASE PRINT)	

Address		Apt. #

City	State/Prov.	Zip/Postal Code

Signature (if under 18, a parent or guardian must sign)

Mail to the **Harlequin® Reader Service:**
IN U.S.A.: P.O. Box 1867, Buffalo, NY 14240-1867
IN CANADA: P.O. Box 609, Fort Erie, Ontario L2A 5X3

Want to try two free books from another line?
Call 1-800-873-8635 or visit www.ReaderService.com.

* Terms and prices subject to change without notice. Prices do not include applicable taxes. Sales tax applicable in N.Y. Canadian residents will be charged applicable taxes. Offer not valid in Quebec. This offer is limited to one order per household. Not valid for current subscribers to Harlequin Special Edition books. All orders subject to credit approval. Credit or debit balances in a customer's account(s) may be offset by any other outstanding balance owed by or to the customer. Please allow 4 to 6 weeks for delivery. Offer available while quantities last.

Your Privacy—The Harlequin® Reader Service is committed to protecting your privacy. Our Privacy Policy is available online at www.ReaderService.com or upon request from the Harlequin Reader Service.

We make a portion of our mailing list available to reputable third parties that offer products we believe may interest you. If you prefer that we not exchange your name with third parties, or if you wish to clarify or modify your communication preferences, please visit us at www.ReaderService.com/consumerschoice or write to us at Harlequin Reader Service Preference Service, P.O. Box 9062, Buffalo, NY 14269. Include your complete name and address.

HSE13R

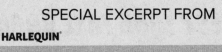
Cecelia Clifton came to Rust Creek Falls hoping to find true love. Then she fell for Nick Pritchett, the commitment-phobic Thunder Canyon carpenter she's known all her life. But when Nick agrees to give his best friend boyfriend-catching lessons, he discovers that there's more to Cecelia than meets the eye—and that he wants her all for himself!

***

"I know these are for the charity auction, but if I give you twenty-five bucks, will you give me a bite of something?"

He must be desperate, Cecelia thought. Plus there was also the fact that she knew that Nick did a lot of charity work. He was always helping out people who couldn't pay him. Her heart softened a teensy bit. "Okay. Two apple muffins for twenty-five bucks. Frosting or not?"

"I'll take one naked," he said and shot her a naughty look. "The other frosted."

His sexy expression got under her skin, but she told herself to ignore it. She handed him a hot cupcake. "It's hot," she warned, but he'd already stuffed it into his mouth.

He opened his mouth and took short breaths.

She shook her head. "When will you learn? When?" she asked and frosted a cupcake, then set it in front of him. "Now that you've singed your taste buds," she said.

He walked to the fridge and grabbed a beer then gulped it down. "Now for the second," he said.

"Where's my twenty-five bucks?" she asked.

"You know I'm good for it," he said and pulled out his wallet. He extracted the cash and gave it to her. "There."

"Thank you very much," she said and put the cash in her pocket.

Within two moments, he'd scarfed down the second cupcake, then pulled a sad expression. "Are you sure you can't give me one more?"

"I'm sure," she said.

He sighed. "Hard woman," he said, shaking his head. "Hard, hard woman."

"One of my many charms," she said and smiled. "You always eat the baked goods I give you in two bites. Don't you know how to savor anything?"

He met her gaze for a long moment. His eyes became hooded and he gave her a smile that branded her from her head to her toes. "There's only one way for you to find out."

***

Enjoy this sneak peek from
MAVERICK FOR HIRE
by New York Times *bestselling author Leanne Banks,*
the newest installment in the brand-new six-book continuity
MONTANA MAVERICKS:
20 YEARS IN THE SADDLE!,
coming in September 2014!

Love the Harlequin book you just read?

Your opinion matters.

Review this book on your favorite book site, review site, blog or your own social media properties and share your opinion with other readers!